What other writer could make you start laughing halfway down the first page of a story about a man putting on a sweater? Thurber maybe, a long time ago. Buy this book.
—Damon Knight, author of *Humpty Dumpty, An Oval*

These stories cannot be compared to anyone else's. There is no one in the same class as Ray Vukcevich. The stories are uniquely, splendidly, brilliantly original, a surprise in each and every one, and brimming with wit and laugh-out-loud humor. A stunning collection.
—Kate Wilhelm, author of *Desperate Measures*

In Ray Vukcevich's ingenious stories the absurd and the profound are seamlessly joined through fine writing. *Meet Me in the Moon Room* is a first-rate collection.
—Jeffrey Ford, author of *The Beyond*

I once heard Ray Vukcevich say about life, humanity, and writing, "All we have is each other." In the spaces between us lie some very strange territories, and this is the ground Ray explores in his stories. There is no other planet like planet Ray; once you visit, you'll want to go back as often as you can. In *Meet Me in the Moon Room*, you get an explosion of guided tours. Grab the bowl with the barking goldfish in it, wind the cat, curl up in a comfortable chair in an abandoned missile silo, and plunge into the wild mind of Ray Vukcevich. No one else can take you on this trip.
—Nina Kiriki Hoffman, author of *Past the Size of Dreaming*

Ray Vukcevich is a marvelous writer. His perspective is skewed, giving us a whole new take on the world. His use of language is unique. And, perhaps most delightful of all, is that Vukcevich stories are completely unpredictable. I envy the person who will be reading Ray Vukcevich for the very first time.
—Kristine Kathryn Rusch, editor of *The Best from Fantasy & Science Fiction: A 45th Anniversary Anthology*

MEET ME IN THE MOON ROOM
:Stories:

MEET ME IN THE MOON ROOM
:Stories:

Ray Vukcevich

Small Beer Press
Brooklyn, NY

Small Beer Press
360 Atlantic Ave., PMB #132
Brooklyn, NY 11217
www.lcrw.net
info@lcrw.net

Cataloging-in-Publication Data
(*Provided by Quality Books, Inc.*)

Vukcevich, Ray.
     Meet me in the moon room / Ray Vukcevich
     -- 1st ed.
     p.cm.
     LCCN 2001087878
     ISBN 1-931520-01-1

     1. Science fiction.   2. Fantastic fiction.
     I. Title.

PS3572.U85M44 2001   813'.54
                        QBI01-700341

First edition 1 2 3 4 5 6 7 8 9 0

Printed with soy inks on 60# Glatfelder recycled paper by Thomson-Shore of Dexter, MI. Text set in Centaur 12 and Missive 18pt. Cover painting by Rafal Olbinski.

:CONTENTS:

For Susan

By the Time We Get to Uranus

Molly had come down with suit in the springtime. What had been a rare and puzzling skin condition a year ago was now an epidemic. People developed space suits, and then they floated off the planet. They usually grabbed whatever stuff was nearby as they left. Molly and Jack weren't much concerned with a cure; there would be no cure for years, if ever. Too late. Sooner or later Jack would be suiting up himself, and that was the problem they were having such trouble talking about. They'd both be going, but they wouldn't be going together.

Jack didn't think Molly's overshoes were fooling anyone. The suit always started with your feet. Everyone knew that. People see a pretty blond woman in a loose red, green, and yellow flowered blouse and big rubber galoshes, they know her skin's got to be going silver, turning to suit, could be halfway up to her butt, you couldn't tell with those relaxed fit jeans she's wearing.

"Everyone's looking at me," Molly said. "I feel like I'm wearing clown shoes."

"No they aren't," Jack said. A lie. "Why don't you sit down here, and I'll go see what we have to do about getting on the plane."

They were flying out of LAX on the way home from a visit with her mother. Molly had told him she needed the trip to say good-bye to everyone else she loved. It had been hard, but they'd done it, and now they were going home to Oregon. Jack came back with the boarding passes and sat down beside her.

"Everyone was gray," she said.

"What?"

"Mom," she said. "You. The neighbors. Everyone. The color of fear is gray. You all try not to show it." She squeezed his hand.

He didn't know what to say. Maybe everyone had been gray. Maybe in some strange way it was the best they could do in sympathy with Molly who was turning silver from the ground up.

She turned her head away, but not before he saw the slow tears. He leaned in and kissed her on the cheek.

"I'm sorry," she said.

"Never mind." He gave her his handkerchief. Say something. Say something. "Seeing your father's trains was pretty neat."

She gave him a weak smile and hugged her canvas bag to her chest. She'd taken one of her father's miniature locomotives, Ol' Engine Number Nine. She'd spent so many happy childhood hours watching her father's trains go around and around and listening to his stories. Molly had been in college when he died. Her mother had left the trains as they were—the track and station and all the little people and cows and, of course, the box cars and locomotives, the Pullman cars, the dining cars, flatbeds and tank cars. The setup was like a shrine, and it embarrassed them both a little, but neither suggested they should box the trains up and put them in storage.

Now Molly would take her favorite locomotive with her when she left the planet.

Boarding for flight 967 to Portland was announced. First class first and folks with babies. Or if you're willing to admit you need some help. They waited.

Then they got on, and he took the window seat. Molly would want to get up. They sat silently waiting for takeoff. He wished she'd look through the in-flight magazine. He wished he could think of something funny or cheerful to say. He looked out the window. They took off.

Flying high in the sunshine at last, Jack saw a wondrous sight, but stopped himself before he could point it out to her—a flock of people in space suits rising up through the smog. They looked as if they'd all been tossed out of a bar together. Tumbling, rolling, twisting. Some hugging their knees. Others stretched out in that optimistic flying superhero posture you so often saw on TV. Others turning head over heels. Cartwheels. And one couple holding hands. How had they managed that?

Oh, look, he almost said, but remembered instead the last flock they'd seen rising. The three of them, Molly, her mother Beth, and Jack, had been drinking ice tea in the glass box that was Beth's balcony overlooking downtown Tarzana. None of them saying much. Being gray, he supposed. Then suited figures rose from somewhere in the urban jumble below. He could see they were not all taking off from the same spot, but they roughly converged without touching before they got very high.

"Why do you suppose that happens?" he asked.

"What?" Beth said.

Molly didn't seem to be paying attention.

"The way they always seem to come together as they leave," Jack said. "You always see groups."

"Actually, if you watch long enough," Beth said, "you see lots of them going alone." She glanced over at Molly, who Jack could now tell from her rigid posture and the red flush around her ears had been paying attention after all. Beth took her hand. "I'm sorry, sweetie."

"There's got to be some way to delay it," Jack said. Maybe if they just got it out in the open. How could you solve a problem if you couldn't even talk about it? "Some way for you to wait for me."

"There's not," Molly said.

"How do you know?"

"There was this thing on prisoners, Jack," Beth said. "On TV."

"What about prisoners?"

"Well, when it's time for them to go, you know, leave this Earth, they have to let them out."

"What happens if they don't let them out?"

Beth looked away. "You don't want to know."

Molly threw her napkin down on the table. "That's just it," she said. "He really does want to know. Everything about this whole business interests him deeply." She pushed away from the table and hurried back inside.

And now on the plane home he watched the flock of suited figures until the plane moved above and beyond them. "Maybe we could stay higher than you need to be until I can catch up," he said.

"What do you mean?" She didn't turn her head to look at him.

"I mean we could hire a plane and fly really high, higher than you'll need to be while I catch up."

"Right." She rolled her head toward him and gave him a tired look. "Maybe we can get the air force to refuel us." She turned away again.

Okay, it was a stupid idea. He was slowly learning to keep his ideas to himself until he'd ironed the wrinkles out of them, but it wasn't easy. Way back when their marriage was young, he'd told her one of the things that made him so crazy in love with her was that he felt free to say stupid things to her. Losing that was hard.

They had gotten rid of Sparky the golden retriever because they were afraid he would jump up on Molly and tear her suit. It would have been nice to come home and be greeted by the animal who had never really been anything but a big puppy. The doghouse with the long lead they'd hooked Sparky to when they got tired of him jumping up on the French doors, begging to get in, remained in the backyard.

At the kitchen table with his morning coffee, Jack looked out at the doghouse and leash and thought that he should move them to the garage, but he thought that every morning. Molly sat in her furry pink robe, slouched over a bowl of cereal. He didn't think she was really eating it.

He picked up the paper again. "Hey, listen to this," he said. "Blah blah blah and on the question of why you get air and pressure and temperature control, not to mention food, water, and waste disposal, the answer is that the good stuff comes from one parallel universe and the bad stuff gets dumped into another."

"I like the one about how we're the cheap fish that God put on Earth to condition the tank," Molly said, "and now we're being pulled off so he can put in a more exotic and interesting species."

Jack lowered the paper. "You really don't care how it all works, do you."

"I really don't care, Jack," she said.

The last time they'd made love, he had joked and called her Barbarella in her silver thigh-high boots. She hit him and laughed, hugged him and cried softly on his chest.

Okay, so how about this? Jack is entirely in his head now, discussing his new idea with a mental construct that looks just like today's Molly, but listens like the old Molly. He might even be asleep at his desk where he was still going over sources on suiting when she wandered off to bed.

We make a small cut. Who knows what's under there? Don't you want to know? If it's really skin, it'll heal. It won't hurt. You said so yourself.

But what if it doesn't heal, Jack? What if there is still a tear and I'm leaking in space. I can't be leaking in space.

That's another thing, he says, just how do you, how do we, well, take a leak in space?

All the comforts of home, Jack.

Maybe I'll make the cut when I have a suit of my own.

Don't do it, Jack.

Just a little cut. There just above your knee.

Bright red blood rises from the razor-sharp slice in the silver fabric.

"Jack."

"Hmm?"

"Jack, please."

Jack jerked up from the desk and looked up at her standing in the doorway of his office. Backlighted from the living room, she seemed to be nude. At least on top.

"What is it?" He got to his feet and came around his desk. There had been something desperate in her tone.

She took his hand and put it on her stomach. "Look here." He could see the very top of the light patch of pubic hair and then silver. He touched the seam lightly. It felt like a cold scar.

"And here." She moved his hand to the top of her left hip. Silver fingers of suit fabric spread into the small of her back. Molly's space pants were complete.

"My guess is a catheter," she said. "Now will you shut up about it?"

The suit had crept up her abdomen to just below her breasts.

"It's possible," he said, "that our universe has touched another somehow and the very different physical rules of the two universes have gotten all jumbled together."

"That must be it," Molly said.

"Or maybe everyone over here with a suit has a double without a suit over there, and somehow what's happening here has metaphorical significance over there."

Molly rolled her eyes, turned and headed for the door.

"Look here," he said quietly, finally giving up on working his way up to it.

Something in his tone stopped her. "What is it, Jack?"

He had his shoe off and his foot in his lap. She approached and dropped down on her knees in front of him. He pulled the big toe of his right foot away from the others. "There," he said, "can you see it?"

A patch of suit.

"I'm so sorry, Jack," she said. She hugged his foot to her cheek and then kissed his toes.

Plan B was a shortwave radio. A ham rig. Transmitter, receiver—the works. He didn't bother with a license. If everything else failed, maybe he could at least stay in touch with her until she drifted out of range.

It turned out Jack was not the only one with such a plan. The guy at the radio place told him he was lucky he hadn't waited another week or he might not have been able to pick what he wanted right off the shelves.

"How will I know where to tune in?" Jack asked.

"Suit communication happens on two frequencies," the clerk said in a tone implying Jack had either been living in the wilderness or was an idiot.

"And those are?"

"HF One and HF Two."

"I don't see anything like that on the dial," Jack said.

"You wouldn't," the clerk said. "I'm talking about Holy Frequency One and Holy Frequency Two. No one knows why God needs two."

Jack pushed his credit card across the counter and glanced at the door to make sure he was clear to make a break for it if necessary. "Do you suppose you could give me the actual numbers?"

The clerk ran Jack's card through the machine. "Sign here," he said.

Jack signed. The clerk took the pen back and wrote the holy frequencies on Jack's receipt.

"Thank you." Jack picked up his boxes. He supposed he had been aware, in some detached way, of the world going crazy around him, but he had been entirely zeroed in on Molly. He hurried home to her.

"There's got to be a way to slow you down," he said. "Or speed me up. I simply cannot accept the scenario where I'm drifting along through space behind you just out of radio range until we get to Uranus."

"Urine nus," she said. "You pronounce it like we all pee."

"You say urine nus," he sang. "And I say your anus."

He'd made her smile. It felt wonderful.

"So why Uranus?" she said.

"I read where someone worked it all out," he said. "The speed we'll be traveling, everything. There's a window. People leaving during this window will just cross the orbit of Uranus in time to be captured by the gravity of the gas giant."

"And what about the people who left before or leave later?"

"They go to Saturn," he said, "or maybe Neptune. Who knows? Some might miss planets altogether."

"And does this genius say why the gravity of Uranus and the other planets will be working any better than the gravity of Earth?"

"It just will be, that's all," Jack said. "What I want to talk about is figuring out a way to go together." He took her hand. "If I miss Uranus, Molly, I could go to Pluto."

Her suit would cover her shoulders soon. He still had only boots and pants not up to his knees.

"I'm already feeling light, Jack." She squeezed his hand. "I don't want to spend these last few days working on a problem we can't solve."

"But . . ."

"I can't feel you," she said. She pulled his hand up to her face. "Touch me here. I want to feel your skin."

"Maybe I could buy an ordinary space suit," Jack said. "And put it on and hold onto you. We both shoot into space and when my skin suit is finished, I just throw away the store-bought one?"

Molly had gotten her helmet that morning. Jack's pants weren't even done yet.

Now she snatched Ol' Engine Number Nine from the kitchen table. "Hold me," she said. "I think something's happening."

He pulled her in close, still muttering nonsense about his latest plan. Her faceplate snapped into place. The sound startled him and he nearly jumped away from her, but then he saw the fear in her eyes behind the glass and held on tight. She went weightless in his arms.

Then she was more than weightless. He could feel her tugging to get higher. He was having trouble holding her down. She slipped away from him and her head bounced lightly against the ceiling. She drifted toward the French doors. He grabbed her foot.

She dragged him toward the doors.

"It hurts." She might have been shouting, but her voice was muffled. "I need to go up, Jack."

"Not yet!"

She parted the French doors with both hands, threw them open wide, and dragged him out into the backyard. He took giant steps, dream leaps, as she pulled him off the ground. He would have to let her go.

Then he saw Sparky's leash. He got a good grip on her ankle with one hand and stretched down for the leash. The grass had grown up around it. Had it been that long? Just a few more inches. No, he couldn't reach it. Desperately he hopped toward the doghouse. The force pulling her into space was getting stronger. He would have only one more chance.

He got to the doghouse in another two big leaps and hooked his foot into the door and pulled down with his leg. He got the other foot hooked in too, and pulled with both legs. Molly came down. Jack reached down with one hand and grabbed Sparky's leash. He maneuvered it through his fingers until he found the end. Her pull was very strong now. If he didn't get her tied down in just the next few moments, he would lose her.

He looped the leash around her ankle and his other hand. He pulled himself closer and took the leash in his teeth. Then with his free hand and his teeth, he tied a clumsy knot. It wouldn't hold, but it wouldn't have to hold long. He let go of her leg and grabbed the leash with both hands and secured the knot.

Jack fell back onto the ground and Molly shot off for space. He heard her cry out when the leash stopped her with a snap. She floated above the backyard like a tethered balloon. He thought crazily that the neighbors would think this was some kind of advertising gimmick. What would they think he was selling?

When he noticed the doghouse lifting off the ground, he grabbed and secured the other end of Sparky's leash to a water spout and left Molly tethered and moving one arm slowly up and down like she was pointing at something. She seemed bigger, bulging. He needed to talk with her.

The shortwave rig was in his office. He had thought she'd already be out of sight by the time he used it. He would be in his office surrounded by his books. He would read her things. They would talk.

She would tell him what she saw. Now he needed the radio in the backyard. She was right there. He couldn't just go into his office where he could not see her.

Molly hung motionless now at the end of the leash, and it was like looking down at her dangling from a cliff rather than stretching up toward space.

"Molly!" He yelled. No response.

Jack ran into the kitchen and got the long black extension cord they used to power the stereo when they had backyard parties. He hauled the radio gear out of his office and set it up on a TV tray and plugged it in.

He pulled up a chair and put on the big earphones. He pulled the microphone in its black plastic stand in close and turned the dial to Holy Frequency One. "Molly? Come in, Molly. Can you hear me, Molly? Come in."

Nothing.

He tried Holy Frequency Two.

Still nothing.

If God did speak now, Jack would have to tell Him to get off the air. He needed to talk to Molly.

He stood up and yanked on the leash trying to get her attention. After maybe a dozen tugs, he saw her bend her head down to face the ground. The effort seemed monumental. He waved his arms at her and jumped up and down.

"Is your radio on?" he shouted and pointed at his ears. "Your radio!"

He sat back down in front of his microphone and put the earphones on again.

He found her on Holy Frequency Two.

"Molly!"

"Jack," she gasped. "My foot. I think the pull is getting so hard it will pull my foot off. The prisoners. Remember? Flattened sticky goo on the ceiling. Did mother describe it to you? I think you'll have to let me go, Jack."

She gasped in pain again and dropped Ol' Engine Number Nine. The miniature locomotive bounced onto the lawn.

"Oh, no, Jack."

Jack leaned over and picked it up. He stood up and lobbed it back up at her. She snatched at it, but it slipped through her fingers and fell again.

"This can't be happening," he shouted into the microphone. "It can't be real. The pieces don't fit together quite right. There are too many loose ends! Nothing is working right. There must be something else to try. I can figure it out. Wait, Molly. Just hold on a little longer."

He grabbed the train and threw it up at her.

She missed it again.

"Oh, cut me loose, Jack," she said. "Just cut me loose."

Then she screamed. She seemed to be elongating like a victim on the rack in an old movie, and he couldn't stand the sound of her pain. He ripped off the earphones and ran to the end of the leash.

For an endless moment he couldn't get it untied and didn't know what to do. Then he took a deep breath, took out his Swiss Army knife and carefully opened the big blade.

He cut the leash.

Molly shot into the air.

Jack scrambled back to his earphones. ". . . love you, Jack." And then she was gone.

Jack made careful preparations for his own departure. He would take her train, of course, but he also had a few other supplies. A flashlight for one thing. If you were going to be floating through the deep darkness to Uranus, you'd want to be able to shine a light around and see what was what. The *Collected Works*. And a small fire extinguisher.

"By the time we get to Uranus, there'll be all this junk floating everywhere." The Earth was a big wet blue marble, and he was already talking to himself. "All the stuff people grabbed when they floated away. We'll need to assign clean up crews to pick it all up. Or maybe we can just rearrange it. Who knows maybe someday there will be so much you can see the rings of Uranus from Earth not that there will be anyone on Earth by that time. But you know what I mean."

"Do you know how far away Uranus is?" Not Jack. A voice on his suit radio.

"Well, now that I can no longer touch it . . ."

Hoots. Jeeze Louise. Who is this joker?

Then he saw them. Suited figures scattered around him, the closest waving his arms like a mechanical man maybe a hundred yards away, the sun gleaming in his faceplate.

"My name is Jack," he said, "and like all of you, I'm on my way to Uranus."

"I think we're too late for Uranus," someone said.

"So, here we are zooming along at what? Maybe a hundred miles an hour?" someone else said.

"Oh, surely much faster than that."

"Do you have any idea of how long it would take to get to Uranus, Jack?"

"I really don't think I want to know that," Jack said.

He got a firm grip on Ol' Engine Number Nine, switched on his flashlight, and activated the fire extinguisher which increased his velocity considerably.

THE BARBER'S THEME

Brenda shuddered when old Milo Durkovich lurched into the barbershop. She'd have to clip his nose hairs, and his nostrils were as big as her thumbs. She hated that. Harvey, her boss, beamed a tight-lipped glare her way, and she coerced a smile onto her face.

"Morning, Mr. Durkovich," she said, dusting the red leather seat of her barber chair.

Durkovich made a sound, an East European snort, she thought, or maybe he'd just hacked up pieces of his lungs and then politely swallowed them. He shrugged out of his long black coat, and his sour smell rushed up at her, pushing away the pervasive odors of hair tonic, shaving lotion, and old magazines as he settled into her chair. He smelled like a dead man, she thought, a sweaty dead man, stuffed with garlic sausages and lately reanimated by Frankenstein's spark so he could stumble into Harvey's to have his thin black and white hair trimmed, the black holes of his nose snipped clean.

For one wild moment she thought of draping her green cloth over his head instead of his chest and lap. Call the paramedics! He just sat down in my chair and died, Officer. Can't you smell him?

The picture of Mr. Durkovich sitting there, his head covered with her barber bib, wondering what the hell was going on, getting steamed, made her smile for real. No way she could do it, though. Harvey still had his eye on her. He'd made no bones when he'd hired her. It's your butt, he'd said, my old farts will love your butt. Smile. Be friendly. She'd been that hungry, that broke. Most afternoons, a group of Harvey's customers lounged around the shop, peeking over their magazines to see her stretch and bend, wiggling their bushy eyebrows up and down at her.

Maybe Durkovich would die before she had to pick around in his nose with her scissors.

"Little off the top and sides, Mr. Durkovich?"

"Why ask?"

Cosmetology! What a stupid word. Opportunities limited only by your imagination. Brenda supposed her imagination had hotfooted it to Kenya with Lyle, the poet, the bastard, when he left her with both halves of the rent to pay. I'm leaving you for purely philosophical reasons, he'd said. What could that possibly mean? She didn't know, and she still owed over a thousand dollars on her beauty school tuition. Brenda couldn't afford to lose this lousy job at Harvey's Barbershop.

Something jumped out of Durkovich's hair as she combed and clipped along the back of his neck. Brenda gasped and leaped back, shaking her hand. The man had bugs!

"What is it?" Harvey moved up close to her. Durkovich twisted his head around to stare at her.

"Nothing," she said and moved back in on Durkovich. Time to bite the bullet. Bugs or not, Harvey would can her in a minute if she made Durkovich mad. Another old guy came into the shop, and

Harvey put good cheer and baseball on his mean face and moved back to stand over his own chair.

Brenda gingerly lifted the hair at the back of Durkovich's neck with her comb. Something moved down there, lots of somethings. Brenda bit her lip and moved her head in a little closer. She swooped down like a hawk to hover at treetop level over a tangled, charred jungle. She didn't see the twisting white lice she'd expected. Instead, little brown monkeys swung from black and white branches and vines, and she could hear them chittering as they jumped from the trees she felled with her scissors. A bright swarm of tiny blue birds rose screeching and veered away from her face. The ground she'd cleared looked like old leather. Dead rivers and deep gullies ran this way and that, around puckered termite hills and ragged bomb craters. Would she find Lyle playing Jungle Jim down there? Her hand shook. He'd always treated her like she didn't know any big words. She didn't think she could stand to see that sad, superior look of his.

Brenda clipped quickly up through the forest, leaving the monkeys behind, and as she moved, the air cooled. The trees were not so thick up here. She heard a tiny roar, and when she'd created a clearing, she saw a crowd of students all waving angry fists and signs at buildings shaped like onions. Fires flickered in alleys. She saw the angry flash of gunfire, and the crowd surged screaming into the trees followed by shouting, shooting uniformed men on horseback. Brenda quickly followed with her scissors, north. She had to get out of town fast.

She left Moscow to its rioting and moved toward the top of the world. Up here the ground was dead white; it was, in fact, snow, Brenda realized. The wasteland. Where they send you if you don't know just the right things to say.

Her song, her theme, her favorite music from her all time favorite movie drifted in the frigid air. She snipped down trees across the top of the world in a frantic search for its source. She cut a swath sideways across the world. She cleared paths right down to the snow, some straight as interstate highways, others meandering paths.

Gray wolves followed and watched as two horses dragged a sleigh across a vast empty field of snow. Brenda could see Lara bundled in her white furs, her dark hair blowing around the bottom of her Russian hat. Lara. Brenda. They'd always been one, really. Brenda rubbed her cheek against the thick fur of her coat and looked from where she sat in the sleigh at the smoke rising from the chimney of a lonely cabin in the snow. A man stood in the doorway with his hand raised. She squinted through the blowing snow, her lips trembling and blue with cold.

"Yurii," she whispered.

Siberia and Yurii. Yes. She'd come so far through the snow, endured so much to find him.

He ran through the deep drifts, his ragged coat flapping, his gray leg wrappings dragging at his feet.

"Lara!"

She leaped from the sleigh and rushed toward him. Her theme swelled, filling the air as they met, and he crushed her to his chest. She felt weak and would have fallen in the snow had not his strong arms held her. He pushed her back to look into her face.

He could use a good stylist, she noticed. His hair was a butchered mess. Of course, he had been sick. Long white trenches ran over the top of his head from front to back, from right to left. Sadly, his nose had gotten old. His mustache sprouted from his huge nostrils like evil black weeds.

He put his hands on her shoulders and shook her.

"What's the matter with you!" he shouted in her face.

Brenda slipped from his chest and crumpled at his feet in the hair around her chair.

Yurii Andreievich ran his hands over his head. He looked bewildered.

For a moment, she saw the young medical student who still hid inside that ravaged shell.

"Look what you've done to me, Brenda," he said. "Just look what you've done."

Harvey's face rose like a bad moon behind Yurii's shoulder, and Brenda scooted away from the two men and got to her feet.

She spoke to them with her eyes, said, I have slapped you awake, Yurii, set you free. Take the hand of your new friend, and the two of you run free, laugh and play in the snow. Be happy children.

She slipped off her white barber's smock and handed it to Harvey.

"Hey!"

"Hey!"

Let them spit and sputter. She grabbed her purse and headed for the sunshine.

BEATNIKS WITH BANJOS

Kenneth was seized by invisible forces while he, Rebecca, and the cat they called Lord Byron were sorting socks and drinking eggnog and feeling blue on Christmas Eve. Kenneth had been turning a festive green and red plaid sock rightside out when the tremors hit. He lost all feeling in his hand, but the sock moved anyway, as if his hand were opening and closing and twisting on his wrist like the head of goose. Kenneth could see a quivering yellow tongue and the slick black void of a throat as the creature zoomed in to stop just inches from his face. Red eyes like blood blisters rose from what he supposed were still, at some level, his first and third knuckles, giving the thing an oddly unaesthetic asymmetry.

"I am," said the goose sock, "the Ghost of Christmas Shifted Sideways in Time."

"And I," Rebecca said, "am the Ghost of Maybe We Should Have Gone To My Mother's For Christmas!"

Kenneth looked over at her and saw that she had the mate to his red and green goose creature on her own hand, but on her the sock was just a puppet and the voice was coming from her own mouth. Couldn't she see what was happening to him?

Rebecca grabbed Lord Byron and put a sock over his head. The cat staggered around pawing and singing like a Christmas drunk. "And this is the Ghost of Christmas With A Bad Attitude," she said. Lord Byron hunkered down in the great pile of socks and made a deep and dangerous sound, and Rebecca relented and snatched the sock off his head. He reached out and swatted at the air a couple of times, but then he seemed to forgive and forget and rolled over on his back in the socks.

Kenneth believed that cats were mechanical devices, but he knew better than to voice that opinion aloud. This was probably his most dangerous secret.

"Can we get back to the business at hand," said the Ghost of Christmas Shifted Sideways in Time, and Kenneth dared another look at its terrible face.

"What do you want?" Kenneth asked.

"Disclosure," Rebecca said.

"I've come to warn you of the Curse of Internal Consistency," the ghost said.

"But internal is good," Kenneth said.

"But not when you keep it to yourself," Rebecca said.

"Consistency is good, too," Kenneth said.

"So you're saying I don't make sense?" He recognized that tone. She was gearing up for round two.

"Yes," the ghost said, "internal is good and consistency is good, but they don't go together."

"You mean they are not consistent with one another?" Kenneth asked.

"Exactly," the ghost said. "At some fundamental level, internal consistency is not consistent."

"So, if you've come to warn me off internal consistency and internal consistency is not consistent, what then is the problem?"

"The problem," Rebecca said, "is that you're talking to a sock on your hand and ignoring Lord B and me altogether."

"The problem," the ghost said, "is that even now you're frantically trying to tie all of this together into a system of experience that is consistent with what you foolishly believe the universe is like. You're trying to make sense of it all."

"But that's how we work," Kenneth said. "We find the patterns in chaos. I mean isn't the world full of portent? Isn't every single thing connected and concerned with every other thing? Isn't it true there are no coincidences? Doesn't every little breeze seem to whisper . . ."

"Oh, please!" Rebecca said.

"Doesn't everything mean something?" Kenneth asked.

"Certainly not," the ghost said. "Internal consistency is not good for you. It is a system for rejecting possibilities. It is a straitjacket for the mind. What you're forgetting is that sometimes a cigar really is just a banana."

"What is all this talk of cigars and bananas?" Rebecca, still wearing the mate of the Ghost of Christmas Shifted Sideways in Time, crawled over to Kenneth. "Can't you just say what you mean?"

She snuggled up to his side, but as soon as she touched him, she stiffened like she'd grabbed an electric wire. The sock on her hand jerked her arm up into the air, and Kenneth realized that sometimes a sock wasn't just a sock. The Ghost of Christmas Shifted Sideways In Time and the Ghost of Maybe We Should Have Gone To My Mother's For Christmas twisted together like snakes and rose up and up and around in a kiss high above Kenneth and Rebecca, forcing them together in a face to face confrontation.

They stared into one another's eyes.

"I'm sorry I called your mother an old poop," he said, the close-up of her brown eyes convincing him that he had been in the wrong all along.

"Now that you mention it," she said, "it occurs to me that your remark was the inspiration for me calling you an anal cartoon. I'm sorry, too."

"I'd blocked that part out," he said.

"Maybe I shouldn't have mentioned it again."

"No, I'm glad you did," he said. "I deserved it."

Her eyes invited and he accepted the invitation and leaned in and kissed her.

"Er, excuse me, kids."

They broke the kiss. The ghosts above them leaned over to look down at the new voice. Kenneth and Rebecca turned to look down too, resulting in them being cheek to cheek. They saw that another sock had gotten onto Lord Byron's head and now the sock was talking. The conglomerate creature looked like a cat with the long neck and head of a cobra.

"I am the Ghost of This Particular Christmas," said the cobra cat, "and boy was I feeling insubstantial there for a while! Now it looks like we can dine on impossible things for breakfast after all."

"How do you dine at breakfast?" Rebecca whispered. "And my god, whose arm do you suppose is in that sock?"

"You use a spoon," said the Ghost of This Particular Christmas. "What we need now is a holy contradiction, something to jump you out of the grooves you have so doggedly dug for yourselves. The two of you must become Beatniks with Banjos, or Compassionate Conservatives, or no wait, I've got it—Christian Atheists. That's the ticket. The best of both worlds. Take what you like and leave the rest. Close your eyes and imagine it. Get down in the trenches. Come on, no more fooling around!"

"But doesn't this fast and loose philosophy of yours mean that we can be absolute scoundrels?" Kenneth asked.

"Yes," said the Ghost of This Particular Christmas, "but if you were scoundrels, being internally consistent would just make you more narrow-minded and dangerous."

"But doesn't this mean we can believe whatever we want?" Rebecca asked.

"Yes," said the Ghost of This Particular Christmas, "it means you can believe whatever you want. Who's to stop you?"

Who indeed.

The sudden realization that his mind was his absolutely and that no one was listening in, that no one was clicking a censoring tongue at him from some astral plane washed over Kenneth in waves of freedom, of joy, and he gasped and pulled away from Rebecca and looked into her sparkling eyes and saw that she had made the same glorious realization. You could believe totally in both sides of an argument at the same time!

Green plants sprouted from the carpet like celery and stars filled the windows like flood lights. No, wait! Those were giants, maybe gods, yikes! maybe even aliens grinning and shining flashlights in at them. Heavenly voices sang heavenly songs, and the smell of cinnamon and oregano filled the air.

"Hey," Rebecca said. "Didn't this Epiphany of ours sort of, well, come right out of the blue?"

"I'd say that's where it came from all right," Kenneth said.

The Ghost of This Particular Christmas crawled onto Kenneth's lap, and the three of them, Rebecca and Kenneth and the baby Byron, not to mention the Ghost of Christmas Shifted Sideways In Time and the Ghost of Maybe We Should Have Gone To My Mother's For Christmas, were sufficient for a midnight mass celebrated with celery and flashlights, some soft humming, and unfolded socks.

Later Kenneth leaned down and kissed Rebecca on the cheek and said, "Go call your Mom, before it gets too late, and give her my love."

"I will!" Rebecca said and got up and rushed out of the room. "Then I'll make cookies!" she called.

Kenneth looked at Lord Byron lazily licking himself. "Meanwhile," he shouted back to her, "I'll wind the cat."

FINALLY FRUIT

When Escotilla, Arizona assembled for the feeding, the townsfolk discovered the monster had grown fruit overnight.

Sam Briggs, holding tight to the neck of his beer bottle, stumbled out of the Oxblood Tavern and leaned against the wall. He pushed his crumpled western hat to the back of his head and looked here and there, blinking his eyes as if amazed to come at long last awake and find himself in such a place as Escotilla on a hot August morning.

Escotilla had struggled for years to put Sam Briggs in his place. He was a little too young to be the town drunk. He was much too old to be sowing his wild oats. His father had been the pharmacist, but everyone agreed that Sam would never follow in his father's footsteps. He hung around the Oxblood, drinking beer and pinching the bottom of Lila Moore, who owned the place and still played the bar girl. All anyone could say for sure was that, besides being generally good for nothing, Sam had some secret sin bottled up inside of him—some scar on his soul that he covered with too much beer and too much loud laughter. Pinned down, Sam would have said there was just something he'd forgotten, something right at the tip of his tongue that he couldn't quite put his finger on.

That morning he couldn't shake the feeling that the thing he'd forgotten, the thing that had, in one way or another, determined the course of his life, had to do with the monster and her new fruit.

Squatting in the dusty town square, she looked like a squashed Sumo wrestler with a huge tropical tree growing from the top of her head. Had two big men been able to get close to her, had they dared stand on her massive shoulders, they could not have encircled her shingled, cream-colored trunk with their arms. Her eyes, as big as dinner plates, were closed, but her long lashes fluttered. Her wide mouth hung open a little, and Sam could see the white spikes of her teeth gleaming in the morning sunlight. A family of four could have eaten dinner comfortably around either of her pink splayed feet. Her wiry black and gray hair flowed over her back like dead vines.

Sam watched Mike Mitchell leaning against the rail of the bandstand, his trumpet loose at the end of his arm. Mike squinted up at the bunches of elongated, tapered yellow fruit under the monster's broad green leaves and peach-and-white blossoms. He stroked the mustache at the edge of his upper lip. Mike thought the mustache made him look dashing. Sam thought it made him look slick and untrustworthy. But what the hell? It would be a shame if any of the old gang went and got respectable. As Bandmaster, Mike had come the closest of any of them, but what would the band play this morning? Where would Mike find his inspiration this time?

Up the street, Sam saw Craig Taft and his father, Walter, each struggling with the end of a long pole onto which a big sow had been tied by her legs. They stopped some ten feet in front of the monster and lowered the pig to the ground. Craig's father took a big red-checked handkerchief from his back pocket, mopped his face, and then wandered away to talk to a group of men out in front of Bert's Barber Shop.

Craig knelt and rubbed the sow's belly and sagging teats. Sam knew Craig hated losing one of his pigs, every one of which he'd given a name to, but the monster had to be fed, and it was his turn. Long ago, before they'd taken to feeding her regularly, she had walked, and on those walks, she gobbled up Mr. Ramsey's entire gaggle of geese, a donkey, and little Billy Boshkin. Better she squat rooted in the square.

Sam pushed away from the wall of the Oxblood and walked over to Craig and his snorting sow. Craig was a big man with powerful arms and legs. His wheat-colored hair stuck up in the back, and his face was boyish, somehow sweet. He looked up when Sam touched his shoulder. Tears, like jewels, had gathered at the corners of his eyes. He turned his eyes quickly back down at the sow.

"There, there, Big Betty," he said. "No trouble. You just take it easy, old girl."

Sam squatted down on his heels by Craig. "Something you can do for me."

"Ain't the time, Sammy."

"Got to be now," Sam said. "It's no big deal."

Craig didn't look up from Big Betty's pink and brown speckled belly.

Sam squeezed Craig's shoulder. "How far you figure you could throw me, Craig?"

"Throw you?" Craig, looking interested in spite of himself, turned his face up to Sam.

"Yeah. Well, suppose you was to get down on one knee and cup your hands and I was to come running and you was to, you know, toss me? How far you figure you could throw me?"

"Skinny butt-head like you, Sammy, I could throw to the moon."

"Don't need to go that far." Sam jerked his chin up at the monster's trunk. "Just want to get me one of those bananas."

"You crazy?"

"You know the answer to that one, old son." Sam grinned and punched Craig on the shoulder. "So will you do it? You toss the bacon here. Then real quick-like you kneel, and I come running."

"Don't call her that."

"What?"

"Big Betty. Bacon."

"Yeah, right. Right. Well, will you do it?"

"So, why don't you just wait until she's fed and sleepy and climb up from the back? You could get too high to reach before she knew what was happening."

"Where's the sport in that? Come on, work with me here."

Craig looked around at Escotilla's assembled citizenry. "They ain't gonna like it."

Sam punched him in the arm. "Do they ever? But old Mike there'll like it. Liable to swallow his horn. And Lila." He leered at Craig and wiggled his eyebrows up and down. "You know Lila will get a kick out of it. And you and me'll like it. The Terrible Five ride again!"

"Four," Craig said. "The Terrible Four."

"That's what I said."

"No, you said . . ."

Sam cut him off. "So will you do it?" Craig's father separated himself from his barbershop cronies and ambled back to help toss the pig. "Hurry up, Craig. Tell me you'll do it."

"Your funeral," Craig said, and shrugged.

Sam slapped Craig on the shoulder again and got to his feet. "That's my man." He stepped back to give himself some running room.

Craig's father took up one end of the pole and Craig took up the other. Big Betty struggled and squealed. Mike on the bandstand waved his hands at his ragtag troop of musicians: Spanish guitar, fiddle, French horn, and tuba. He put the trumpet to his lips, and the band leaped, like a startled deer, into a song.

Mike lowered his trumpet and sang: "Yes, she has no bananas. She has no bananas today!"

The monster roared.

Sam put his hands on his knees and got ready to make his mad dash. Craig and his father swung Big Betty—one, two, three. The song tingled through Sam's body. Craig and his father tossed the pig at the monster's gaping meatgrinder mouth.

The pig screamed.

Sam tossed his hat to the ground and ran.

Craig dropped to one knee and cupped his hands.

"She has no bananas today!" Mike sang.

Sam stepped into Craig's hands, and Craig heaved. Sam flew. The monster closed her teeth on the pig, and Big Betty's scream stopped abruptly in a riot of snapping bones and dark blood.

Sam sailed over the monster's terrible face and hit her trunk with a splat. He felt himself slipping, and he clawed at her rough bark.

She must have swallowed the pig or spat it out, because she roared again, and her trunk swayed from side to side as if a hot desert storm had raged up the mountain to blow through Escotilla. Sam scrambled up her trunk for the bunched fruit. Her arms, he knew, could only reach so far.

Maybe far enough. Something scratched down the back of his jeans and snatched at his boots. He looked down and saw her pale white hands, strangely delicate with their long white fingers, clawing for a hold. He climbed out of range.

She stretched up her arms, like sinewy vines, as far as she could, but she couldn't reach him. She shuddered, then quieted and pulled her arms back down. Sam hoisted himself up to her bananas.

There were two bunches, one to the left and one to the right. Like ears, he thought. Little black flies swarmed around the fruit. Sam stretched out one arm and grabbed a banana, and the monster trembled. He pulled but the banana wouldn't break loose. He glanced down and around at the townsfolk. Everyone was silent, watching him, waiting, he thought, for him to make a mistake and fall. Crazy Sam Briggs.

"Okay," he said. "Okay." He jerked at the banana, once, twice, and it came away in his hand. She groaned. Where the banana had been attached, bright red blood gathered and fell in slow drops to the dusty street below.

Sam inched his way up under the hanging fruit until he could wedge himself in, freeing his arms and hands to open his prize. The stem still bled a little, and he bent it to one side. The rind split along the top, and he tugged it away from the fruit inside. More like pulling the skin from a chicken. Inside, the fruit was gray with pale purple veins running through it.

Sam tossed the skin away and raised the warm flesh of her banana to his lips. He closed his eyes and bit and felt her hot blood fill his mouth. Memory leaped up behind his head and banged his face into the tree. He fell into his childhood, into the icy summer flash flood waters roaring down Mad Dog Creek. Sammy, swept along with the red manzanita branches and broken trees of the oak and pine forest, washed ashore by the Witch's cottage, where it had never been before. The cottage must have moved there during the night on those big chicken legs. You never knew where you'd find it.

"It does so have chicken legs! You just can't always see them."

"Baloney," said Lila. And Sammy and Mike and Craig grinned and elbowed one another as the Witch's daughter turned her bright brown eyes up at them.

Julie!

She was so pretty in her satiny black dress, her hair long and blacker than a wet crow's wings, her skin so white, a miniature woman, a porcelain doll with a crooked grin. Julie put her hand on her mouth and wiped the smile from her face and looked at Lila. She made claws of her tiny white hands and wiggled her fingers. "Bibbity bobbity boo, Lila." The blood drained from Lila's face and she took a step back, then another, stumbled, and fell on her butt. What a hoot.

What shall we do, Julie? Let's shake 'em up. What shall we do?

The Terrible Five.

Who TPs the trees? We do!

Who soaps the windows? We do!

Who runs the town ragged?

Who is it? Who is it? The Pharmacist's boy. The Pig Farmer's kid. And that Mike who toots his own horn. And Lila. Lila with the tits, and she's not even ten. Imagine that. And don't forget the Witch's Daughter. The one who's so hard to see. Julie Yaga.

They sat quietly on that stuffy summer afternoon, looking at Julie's head. The cottage was strangely still. Julie stared down at her hands folded in her lap.

"Baba's gone," she said.

"Gone?"

"Bigger fish to fry, she said." Julie looked up at them, and they could see she'd been crying. "She said I'd be fine. Keep sewing, she said."

"But what is that on your head?" Lila demanded.

"I dropped another stitch this morning," Julie said.

"But what is that?" Lila asked again. She reached out but didn't touch.

The boys were curious, too, but they wouldn't ask.

Julie ran the back of her hand under her nose and sat up a little straighter. "I don't know. It was just there this morning."

Sammy moved in closer to look at the little tree rising up through

Julie's black hair. There were little green leaves, just at the top, and tiny white flowers.

"Well, take it off!" Lila said. "It looks stupid. Like a green toilet brush or something."

"I can't." Julie looked sad. "It's growing there."

"Oh, gross!" Lila said. "That's disgusting."

"Hey! I think it's neat." Sam sat down beside Julie and put his arm around her shoulders and hugged her close. "It'll drive 'em crazy in town."

They all got to giggling then. Even Lila joined the group hug.

"They needn't know," Julie said. "No one should know that Baba's gone. They'd take me away if they found out. You'll all forget I said she was gone."

"Sure we will," said Sam.

In the years that followed, the tree grew taller and wider. Julie's neck expanded to the circumference of her head. She had to hold on to things for balance when she walked. Sometimes she needed help. Mike was too busy with his horn, Craig with his pigs, Lila with her tits. Finally only Sam remembered her at all.

"You'll leave me, too, Sammy."

Sam sat tossing rocks into the creek. "No, I won't." He'd been thinking of Lila and the way his head swam when she'd touched him the night before at the Grange dance. He looked away from Julie's squashed features. Her flattening eyes. Her wide mouth always seeming to grin horribly under the weight of her tree. As the tree grew, her body spread. Her legs grew shorter and thicker. She'd developed a smell that reminded Sam of raw chicken.

"Everyone leaves me," she said. "First her, then them, now you."

"You know I love you, Julie," he said, but he said it automatically. He couldn't have said what it meant, unless it described the nagging obligation he felt.

"Maybe you did once," she said. "But it looks like it wasn't enough to stand up to this kind of pain."

"I'm not going to sit here and listen to that kind of stupid talk." He got up and dusted off the seat of his pants. He had brought her food, but he didn't want to stay and watch her tear it to pieces. "I'd better get back."

"Just like I said. You don't want to be around me."

Sam looked up at Julie's tree, and he felt a cold rage twist his guts. "Haven't I spent enough time talking to the trees?"

Julie jerked back and nearly toppled herself. He felt a strange satisfaction at her stricken look.

"The least you could do," he said, "is sprout some fruit."

Julie put her hands over her face and her shoulders shook and her leaves rustled.

"How about bananas?" Sam's rage peaked and he put his hand on Julie's shoulder and pushed.

She sat back hard on the ground, then toppled to the side. She looked up at him. "I thought you were my friend, Sammy." She put her hands over her face and cried.

He was glad he'd hurt her, this creature, this thing that had swallowed his friend and scattered the gang. Together they had had something; separately they were all so ordinary, each of them lining up to be defined, pinned down, understood, and dismissed.

He squatted down in front of her and pulled her hands from her face. "Julie was my friend. You're just something that came out of the woods and stole her."

Julie.

Why do little girls get lost in the woods?

"Sammy!"

She rolled over and pulled her knees in under herself. Her butt rose into the air, but the weight of her tree pinned her face to the mud and wet leaves and pine needles. Her voice was muffled as she struggled and called to him for help.

Sam backed away from her. Somewhere under that mass of muscle and sticks and leaves, Julie sobbed. What had he done? Sam took another step back. He should go to her now. Take it all back. Make it all better.

He turned to run.

Julie roared.

Sam's foot tangled in a deadfall, and he tripped. He snatched at the air and felt something squish between his fingers like the mud of Mad Dog creek. He saw Julie's broad green leaves sweep up and away into the sky as he plunged toward the hard ground of the town square. He heard the townsfolk gasp.

One of her pale hands darted through the air and snagged his ankle. Julie lowered him to hang upside down by one leg in front of her awful face. Her other arm snaked out, and she grabbed his other ankle and scissored his legs open and shut, open and shut. Her lips and teeth were smeared with Big Betty's blood. She closed one eye in a terrible wink, then opened it again. A rumbling came from somewhere deep inside of her.

"Julie," Sam said and let himself go limp. She would crush him like a pig in those huge jaws. It was no more than he deserved.

Julie released one of his legs and took him under the arms and turned him upright. Easily, like a kitten. She shook him a little and pulled him in close. With an effort that twisted her face and pushed her tree higher into the air, she puckered her purple lips. When she kissed him, her kiss covered him from head to toe. Then she put him on his feet and let him go.

Sam stepped away from her. A trembling overtook her, and she shook from the top of her tree down to her feet. Her huge head suddenly moved up the trunk of her tree like an elevator. When it reached the top, her leaves became a thatched roof, and her eyes went blank and became windows and her mouth became a door. Her feet went yellow, grew talons, and her trunk split into two giant chicken legs.

The witch's hut ran out of town, kicking up dust and scattering the crowd, and as it left, Sam thought he saw her in the window, the sudden white flash of her smile, the black shadow of her hair. She would be waiting in the woods.

PRETENDING

The missile silo was Stuart's idea. It was his turn to make up a holiday tradition. The silo belonged to a man named Johnson who had moved his family back to Cheyenne. Johnson and his wife had spent a lot of money fixing the place up, and they'd given it their best shot, but it hadn't taken long to discover that a missile silo was an awful place to raise a family. Now he rented it out to people like Stuart.

The party this year was Stuart and Marilyn, Bill and Elizabeth, and Lewis. Bill was a lawyer and Elizabeth taught math at the same college where Stuart was in Psychology and Marilyn, when she wasn't on sick leave, was a research biologist. Lewis was a computer programmer. Sally was missing this year. She'd left Lewis and gone back to New York in the spring.

Last year it had been Elizabeth's turn to come up with a candidate tradition. She'd taken them to the Mojave where they had jumped out of an airplane. Since none of them had done it before, they jumped in tandem with instructors snugged onto their backs. Lewis had made a lot of bad jokes about being ridden to earth by the sky patrol. The instructors were all getting good xmas eve overtime but none of them seemed happy about it. On the way down, Marilyn had wet her pants and hadn't spoken to any of the others for weeks afterwards.

The year before that, it had been Lewis and snake handling in Louisiana. Marilyn hadn't spoken for a long time after that one, either.

The reason the gang needed to make up a new tradition every year was that they had no traditions of their own. They were neither Christian nor Jewish, neither Muslim nor Hindu. The list of things they were not was very long. They were Americans of a certain class and education, in their forties, atheists or maybe closet agnostics. No children. They felt completely left out of things during the holidays, so they came together to seek out new rituals, new meanings. Over the years the search itself had become the tradition.

This year Marilyn had gotten a head start on not speaking to Stuart. She was turning herself down, speaking less frequently, and with less volume when she did speak. She was as quiet as a mouse on the drive out to the silo, her head resting against the car window until her cheek got too cold and she sat up to stare out at the snow. She looked like a sickly child bundled up in too many winter clothes. She coughed, and her cough was an accusation.

"I'm sorry," she said. "Are we there yet?"

He hadn't told her what he was up to. He knew that telling her would be like telling everyone. Elizabeth would have wheedled it out of her. He wanted it to be a big surprise—the vast plain of snow, the endless drive into nowhere, the headlights finally picking out the wire fence and the shack that must surely be too small to be their destination.

"Yes," he said at last, "we're here."

He and Lewis busted open the frozen door on the shack covering the entrance, and they all climbed down into the silo. Stuart switched on the power and gave them the tour. Here was the control room, now a media center, and here the crew quarters, now cozy bedrooms. Way down there were the spooky storerooms, and all those corridors and huge heavy doors, and, maybe most disturbing, the hole where the intercontinental ballistic missile had been. It was half-filled with water—more than a hundred feet of water, Stuart said, and there were flooded passages, another underwater world down there. Echoes and a slimy green smell. Even with the flashlights it wasn't easy to make out the surface of the water. None of them stayed long at the edge.

He led them back to a room that had once been the crew's mess. He let them bunch up at the door behind him, then stepped aside and switched on the light to reveal a lavishly appointed dinner table.

The walls of the dining room had been papered white with a faint red rose pattern. A picture Stuart had first mistaken for a big photograph mimicked a window on one wall. When he looked a little closer he saw it was a painting. Not a very good painting. He doubted even a very good painting would have chased away the overwhelming sense of being underground. It had something to do with the way light and sound behaved, something about the earthy smell of the air.

"Everyone sit down," he said. "I'll serve the soup."

Once into the soup course, Stuart warmed them up with his "alas, we middle-aged American atheists have no deep traditions" routine. It was the standard opening of their ritual.

"The Catholic Mass or the twelve days of Christmas. Hanukkah or Ramadan. We're excluded from all of that."

"Not excluded," Elizabeth said. "We've opted out."

"Yes," they all said together, like a chant. "Opted out."

"Well, tonight," Stuart said, "we are going to do an exercise in creative belief."

He had their attention. This would be the point of the evening. His proposal was simple.

Just believe something.

He suggested they start with ghosts.

"You're suggesting that if there are no ghosts," Bill said, "we must make our own?"

"Exactly," Stuart said.

"We have met the supernatural," Elizabeth said, "and the supernatural is us?"

"Now you're getting it," Stuart said.

"But why are we doing this?" Lewis asked. "What exactly do we hope to accomplish?"

"I want us to experience what most of the rest of the world claims to experience all the time," Stuart said. "Before the evening is over, I want each of us to know what it is like to believe the unbelievable."

"No matter how hard we try," Marilyn said, "I don't think we'll get ghosts just because we want to." She didn't look up when she spoke.

"You're right," Stuart said. "We are all unapologetic materialists. We'll need a little help." He would say no more until after dinner. No one complained. The delay was part of the ritual, too.

After dinner, they regrouped in the parlor. There was a fake fireplace with an electric fire. There was a round table in the middle of the room. On the table was a single black candle. To one side was a bar. Lewis spotted it at once and poured himself a drink.

"What?" he said when he caught them all looking at him.

"I have picked ghosts for us to believe in," Stuart said, "because I think we can use a mental aid that will make it easier."

Bill joined Lewis at the bar and mixed a drink for himself. He raised an eyebrow at Elizabeth but she shook her head no.

"We'll have to make our own ghost," Stuart said. "You can think of it as a game. The game for tonight. The main event. One of us will become a ghost. The degree to which that person becomes a ghost will depend on how strongly the rest of us believe that person is a ghost."

"You're talking about me," Lewis said.

"Why you?" Stuart asked.

"Odd man out."

"Actually," Stuart said, "I was thinking we'd draw straws. Look, I've already set it up. Short straw is the ghost." He took the straws he had prepared earlier from his jacket pocket.

"Here, you go first, Marilyn." He pushed the straws in front of her face. "Go on, pick one."

She sighed and took a straw. He saw that she had gotten the short one. He hadn't exactly planned it that way. In fact, he had been holding back. He knew how to force a card or, in this case, a straw. He had learned that trick in a psych course taught by a magician when he was a grad student, but he didn't think he'd used it on Marilyn. No one else knew the rest of the straws were redundant, so he went through the entire exercise letting each of them pick one. There was one left in the end for him. He held his up and everyone did the same. It was easy to see that Marilyn would be the ghost.

"Our ghost person, let's call her Marilyn." He smiled at her. "She is merely a focus of attention. After all, what is a ghost but the point of concentrated desire?"

"Fear?" Lewis asked. "Concentrated fear?"

"In the unlikely event that this works," Bill said, "I mean, if I can convince myself that Marilyn really is a ghost, then she'll disappear."

"Why disappear?" Elizabeth asked.

"Because I don't believe in ghosts," Bill said.

"You mean, if you believe Marilyn is a ghost, you won't be able to see her, because you don't believe in ghosts?"

"You got it," Bill said. "It's a Zen of Physics kind of thing."

They were talking about Marilyn as if she weren't there, Stuart thought. It was working already. He hated to break the momentum but he needed to get her moving. She wouldn't be much fun as a ghost if she just sat there looking ill and pathetic. "Let's get this show on the road," he said. "Marilyn?"

"What do you want me to do?" Her voice wasn't much more than a whisper.

"Be a ghost," Stuart said. "You've got this ideal spooky place to haunt, so go haunt. Pass on to the other side. We'll light the candle and sit around the table and hold hands and call you back with pure belief."

Marilyn pushed herself up out of her chair and walked to the heavy metal door. Her shoulders slumped as if she were thinking she'd never be able to get it open, but then she must have remembered the doors were perfectly balanced because she grabbed the wheel and pulled. The door swung aside smoothly and she moved into the corridor.

"Okay," Stuart said. "Let's take our places at the table."

"What is this?" Bill sounded irked, but Stuart had known him long enough to know that he was intrigued.

"Mood," Stuart said. He lighted the candle and switched off the electric light. "Believing the unbelievable is all about mood. Come on, sit down."

Bill and Elizabeth took chairs at the round table. Lewis filled his glass again and sat down next to Elizabeth.

Stuart sat down. "Okay, hold hands."

"Oh, boy," Elizabeth said. She took Bill's hand. Lewis was staring down at his drink and didn't respond to her outstretched hand.

"Come on, Lewis," Stuart said.

"Okay, okay," Lewis said. "Let's blast off." He took Elizabeth's hand.

"Everyone close your eyes," Stuart said.

"Studies show that listening to Mozart strengthens your mind," Bill said.

"Personally, I go for Ginkgo Biloba," Elizabeth said.

"All you need is love," Lewis said, maybe a little bitterly.

"Close your eyes, and she will come," Stuart said.

One by one they closed their eyes. Stuart closed his last. He waited. Bill's hand was dry. Lewis' was cold from the ice in the drink he'd been holding. Stuart's chair was hard.

"Do you think we should say her name in spooky voices?" Elizabeth asked.

"No," Stuart said. "Maybe. I don't know. Let's try concentration first."

He concentrated.

Several minutes later, he peeked out at the others and looked right into the wide-open eyes of Elizabeth. She gave him a crooked grin and a wink. He frowned at her, and she sighed and closed her eyes. He waited a moment more to make sure everyone was cooperating before closing his eyes again.

"Maybe we should turn up the fire," Lewis said.

"Quiet," Stuart said.

It did seem colder. And the underground sounds, the pressure of all that earth and snow above, seemed to press down a little harder. He imagined the room had gotten smaller. If he opened his eyes now, he would see the walls just a few inches from the table. Marilyn would be there like an unhappy spirit—always hanging around hoping, on the one hand, she wasn't bothering anyone, and weepy, on the other hand, because she was unable to have much impact on the living. He could see the flickering candlelight through his eyelids.

Then there was a breeze.

Of course, there could be no breeze in the silo. This was a breeze produced by his belief. It was the wind that would blow the ghost of his dead wife into the parlor of the ICBM silo. There was a rustle of cloth, like the thighs of someone sneaking around in tight jeans. Then tiptoes through dead leaves.

The breeze became the gentle huff of breath on his cheek.

Someone whispered, very close, her lips just brushing his ear, "Both sexes of alligators bellow."

It didn't sound like Marilyn, and certainly not like anything Marilyn would say. She might have been like that a long, long time ago. Bright eyes and big smile, and the way she had moved just made your fingers itch to unwrap her, but nothing like that these days. These days she was the coughing woman. The whimpering woman. The I-don't-mean-to-bother-you-but-I-must-moan woman. Both sexes of alligators bellow. Such a wet thought. And there was the smell of lemons.

Elizabeth gasped. Then there was silence again. Stuart listened carefully but he couldn't be sure he wasn't imagining the sounds of something drifting around the table delivering little messages from the great beyond.

He wanted to see her.

He opened his eyes. Marilyn wasn't in the room. Bill's chin had tipped down to his chest. He might have fallen asleep. Elizabeth, her eyes squeezed tightly shut, was sitting up very straight and seemed to be struggling to hear something. Slow tears streaked Lewis' cheeks.

Where had Marilyn gone? Had she been there at all? The entire point of the supernatural was the willingness to fool yourself. So had he succeeded in fooling himself about the breeze and the lips on his ear and the voice? He cleared his throat.

Bill sighed and raised his head. Elizabeth opened her eyes. Lewis pushed up from the table and turned away.

"Well, that was weird," Bill said.

"Where's Marilyn?" Elizabeth stood up.

"I'm wondering the same thing," Stuart said.

Lewis poured himself a fresh drink. "Maybe she just went to bed," he said without turning back to them.

Stuart looked around the dining room and then the rooms immediately connected to it, but Marilyn was not to be found.

"Frankly, I'm a little worried," Elizabeth said. "She did look pretty green even before she became a ghost."

"Okay," Stuart said. "Let's split up and look for her."

"That's what they always say in the movies," Lewis said.

"Oh, shut up, Lewis," Elizabeth said.

Outside in the corridor there was a hum that Stuart hadn't noticed before. Maybe he had not been perfectly still and listening before. "I'll go this way," he said.

He checked all of the rooms and passages on his way to the missile hole. When he got to the hole itself and saw her standing there in the wedge of light from the corridor, he was surprised at how unsurprised he was. She had changed into her nightgown and white silk robe. She was barefoot and her feet were faintly blue. She was looking straight at him. She hardly ever looked straight at him these days. Maybe becoming a ghost had given her new knowledge, new strength, a kind of cosmic aikido. He approached her. If he were to reach out and touch her, his hand would pass right through her.

He put out his hand and pushed. She fell back into the hole. A moment later he heard the splash.

In a single instant, belief became reality. He turned away and moved to the door. She might have been feebly calling his name had she really been down there, but she wasn't really down there. Marilyn couldn't swim which was probably why they had not yet swum with the sharks on xmas eve. She wouldn't be anywhere near a hole filled with maybe a hundred feet of cold water. He closed the corridor door and walked slowly back toward the dining room.

You can believe your life into any state you want, he decided. Reality is plastic. You mold it. You pretend things into existence.

There would be big changes to make back home. He'd take some time off school, surely all of next term. Maybe go to Europe to get over this.

Maybe buy a BMW.

Bill came out of the shadows like a sudden psycho. He had a crazy grin on his face.

"Bill," Stuart said.

"We found her," Bill said. "Hey, here she is now."

Elizabeth came into the corridor pushing Marilyn in ahead of her. Lewis appeared with his drink.

"Safe and sound," Elizabeth said.

Marilyn's feet were still blue. She still wore her white silk robe over her nightgown.

"Doesn't she make a good ghost?" Elizabeth said.

Marilyn didn't speak but she didn't turn her eyes down either.

"Well, it's been fun, kids," Bill said, "but I'm for bed."

"Me, too," Elizabeth said quickly.

"Not me," Lewis said.

"Oh, you can stay up all night drinking if you want," Elizabeth said.

Marilyn moved away down the corridor toward the bedrooms. Stuart followed. What else was there to do?

Once in the bedroom, he sat down on the bed and tugged off his shoes. Marilyn hadn't moved away from the door. He could feel her eyes on him, but when he looked up at her, she switched off the light, leaving nothing but an afterimage of sadness and contempt.

He could hear water dripping on concrete.

He felt buried alive in the absolute darkness. Was she still there by the door? Had she ever really been there?

"Say something," he said.
Nothing.
"Please," he said.
Maybe he had imagined her, after all.
"Boo," she said.

Mom's Little Friends

Because he wouldn't understand, we left Mom's German shepherd Toby leashed to the big black roll bar in the back of Ada's pickup truck, and because Mom's hands were tied behind her back and because her ankles were lashed together, we had some trouble wrestling her out of the cab and onto the bridge.

My sister Ada rolled her over, a little roughly, I thought, and checked the knots. I had faith in those knots. Ada was a rancher from Arizona and knew how to tie things up. I made sure Mom's sweater was buttoned. I jerked her green and white housedress back down over her pasty knees. I made sure her boots were tightly tied.

The breeze sweeping down the gorge made the gray curls above her forehead quiver. The wind seemed to move the steel bridge a little, too, but that may have been my imagination. Even from up here, I could smell the river and hear its gravelly whisper. Black birds circled and complained in the clear blue sky above us. The sun was a hot spotlight in the chilly thin mountain air. Toby paced back and forth in the truck bed, whining and pulling at his leash and watching us closely.

"What about the glasses, Barry?" Ada tapped a fingernail on the lenses of Mom's fragile wire-rimmed glasses.

"Please, don't do this, children."

"Shut up, Jessica." Ada spoke not to our mother but to Mom's interface with her nanopeople. When Dr. Holly Ketchum (Mom, that is) introduced a colony of nanopeople into her own body, it was seen by many as a bold new step. It had, after all, never before been done under controlled conditions. Nanotechnology held such promise—long life and good health, a kind of immortality, really.

So how did it work out? What one word would sum it all up?

Well, "whoops" might be a good choice.

The problem was that after a few generations, that is to say, after a few hours, the nanopeople became convinced that their world shouldn't take any unnecessary chances. It made no sense to the nanopeople to let their world endanger herself. Jessica claimed that individually, nanopeople were as adventurous as anyone else. "But put yourself in our place, Barry," she'd once said to me. "Would you let your world put sticks on her feet and go speeding down a snowy mountain at 60 miles an hour? Or swim with sharks? Be reasonable."

Mom looked like a TV grandmother these days—plump, rosy cheeks, and translucent white skin. Her nanopeople could have fixed her vision easily enough, but they thought the glasses would make her more cautious in most situations. They could have left her appearance at its natural 48 years or even made her look younger, but they chose this cookie-cutting, slow-shuffling granny look to discourage relationships that might turn out to be dangerous. They could have left her mind alone; instead they struck her silly. A slow-moving stupid world is a world that takes no chances.

Jessica had been created to explain things to Mom. She was really a network of nanopeople working in shifts to produce the illusion that called itself Jessica. The nanopeople, invisible, sentient, self-replicating robots of nanotechnology, simply thought more quickly than big people. If Mom were struggling to access a multi-syllabic word, there could be a week's worth of shift changes among the nanopeople running the Jessica interface. In fact, a nanoperson could come into existence, grow up, get trained, find a mate, write poetry, procreate, rise to the top of a career, screw up a relationship, get cynical, and die in the time it took Mom to cook up a batch of brownies.

The real horror, I suppose, was that while individual nanopeople might come and go, as a society, they intended to keep Mom alive and stupid pretty much forever.

I plucked the glasses from her face. "I'll save these for you, Jessica, just in case you ever need them again." I gave her a look I hoped was menacing and let my remarks just sit there for a moment, then I sat Mom up and leaned her against the bridge railing. "There's still time for negotiation, Jessica," I said.

"I'm sure I don't know what you mean, Barry." Jessica was doing what the nanopeople thought was Mom's voice. I wasn't fooled. Mom never whined. Not the old Mom anyway. At least we had the nanopeople's attention these days. At first, Jessica had not bothered to even acknowledge our existence. Then we started pushing Mom into water over her head, and Jessica decided to talk to us.

I tied the big rubber bands to Mom's boots.

"The word is *bungee*, Jessica," Ada said.

My sister was becoming one scary chick, I thought, what with her horse tattoo and western hat and the ever-present toothpick in the corner of her mouth. It was almost like she was enjoying this. Or maybe she was just a better actor. I remembered how she'd cried on the phone the night she called me home from graduate school in Oregon, how she kept saying Mom had nothing on her mind but cookies, cookies and cakes and those little flaky things with sweet red crap in the middle, and I need your help Barry, I can't do this alone Barry. I'd gotten verbal assurance from my advisor in the physics department that I could take a leave of absence and had bussed to Tucson the very next day.

Mom made me a pie when I got home.

I took Mom under the arms, and Ada grabbed her feet. We swung her like a sack of laundry, and on the count of three, tossed her over the side of the bridge. Toby went crazy, barking and pulling at his leash, in the back of Ada's truck.

We put our hands on the bridge rail and watched Mom fall and fall toward the river, the long bungee bands trailing behind her, and listened to her scream—well, listened to someone scream, anyway; when it was Jessica, it was a howl of frustration and terror, but when it was Mom, it was an exuberant whoop! Or maybe I was imagining things. Maybe I didn't have the faith Ada had in this plan to get the nanopeople out of Mom.

We watched Mom bounce like a yo-yo on the end of her bungee bands, her housedress hanging down over her head. We decided to let her swing awhile. Ada unpacked our picnic lunch and we settled down on the bridge to eat.

As we munched and sipped, I heard a small voice calling, "Help, help," but I decided to ignore it.

"So, Ada," I said. "How come Mom's nanopeople don't transform her into something that can climb up the rubber bands? A giant spider, say."

"I call the answer to that my King Kong Theory," Ada said. "I'll bet the nanopeople can see in Mom's memory that picture of Kong on the Empire State Building with all the airplanes buzzing around and shooting. Or some other picture like that. The thing with these guys is safety first and always."

Those far away cries for help were getting to me. I gave Ada a sidelong glance. I didn't want my big sister to think I was wimping out on her. "So, shall we pull her up?" I tried to sound casual.

"I suppose." Ada took another bite of her sandwich then tossed it into the basket.

We pulled Mom up.

"So, Jessica," Ada said. "You want to do that again?"

"No!"

"Let's talk then."

Jessica let Mom's chin fall to her chest and was quiet for a minute or so. Then she raised Mom's head. "What do you want? How can we make you stop this?"

"Get out of Mom!" I shouted, and Ada gave me a sharp look. I had no talent for diplomacy.

"That's pretty much what we want, Jessica," Ada said. "We need to discuss the terms of your eviction."

"That is an absurd notion," Jessica said. "Each one of us lives a life every bit as important and significant as yours, Ada. You just move more slowly. You're just bigger. None of that signifies. Have you no empathy? Holly is our world. This is the only world the People have ever known. Just where do you suppose we could go?"

"We have an idea about that." Ada signaled me with her eyes.

I got up and walked to the truck and untied Toby's leash. With a great leap of joy, he bounded out of the bed of the truck. Tail wagging, trying to look everywhere at once, nose to the ground, nose in the air, he dragged me back to Mom and Ada. I convinced him to sit down in front of Mom. Taking advantage of the fact that she was tied up, he licked her face. I often wondered whether the dog knew this was Mom. He seemed to like this dowdy little person, but this person was always around these days, and it seemed to me his enthusiasm for her was somehow of a lower quality than the worship he had always had for Mom. Maybe he'd just gotten used to Jessica.

"We want you to move to Toby," Ada said.

Toby's ears stiffened at the sound of his name, and he looked up at Ada.

Jessica was quiet for a moment. Then she made Mom's soft grandmother mouth a hard line. "You want us to move into a dog?" She sounded incredulous.

"You got it," Ada said.

"You want an entire civilization, billions of us, each with definite ideas and hopes and dreams, to just shuffle off to another world? You think that generations of tradition and deeply felt religion and philosophy can be tossed aside? You think we'll move into a dog?"

"I think she's got it," Ada said.

"We won't do it," Jessica said. "And we won't discuss it further." She closed Mom's mouth and squeezed Mom's eyes tightly shut.

"Hey! Wait a minute!" I yelled.

"Never mind, Barry." Ada grabbed Mom's feet and gave me a sharp look.

I got the message. I took Mom under the arms, and we tossed her over the side again. Toby just sat there for a moment like he couldn't believe his eyes, then he jumped up and put his front paws up on the railing and watched Mom bounce.

When we pulled her up this time and propped her against the bridge railing, I looked closely into her wild eyes, hoping, I guess, for a little momness. Not a chance. It was clear we'd finally pissed off her little friends. Big things were happening in Mom. Her face twisted into a horrible grimace, her cheeks puffed out and her eyes bulged. She suddenly spit a huge stream of green stuff at us. We jumped out of the way.

"She's mine." The voice was deep and male, a truly scary demon voice. "You can't have her."

"Ah, Jessica," Ada said. She took off her cowgirl hat and used it to swat Mom on the side of the head. "We've seen those movies, too. If you're not going to be serious, we're going to throw you over again."

"You don't know what you've done," Jessica said in her usual Jessica voice. "There have been uprisings since we talked last. People have died. Listen to me, Ada. Barry. People have died. People every bit as real as you. Good people. How can you continue this?"

"But you're destroying our mother!" I said.

"One person for the good of billions! And besides she wouldn't be destroyed."

"This one person is our mother," Ada said. "And that's where you're in trouble. We won't quit. Mom would rather be dead than stupid. Let's throw her over again, Barry."

"Wait!" Jessica said. "That's not true. What you just said. You forget we're inside here. We have access that you don't have. We talk to Holly all the time. We're not monsters. Holly is our Mother World."

"Then why do you keep her stupid?" Ada asked.

"Not stupid." Jessica sounded sincere, but I didn't buy it. "Content. Holly is our mother, but she is also our child to be guided, much as you mold and guide your own world."

I could have told her a thing or two about how well we molded and guided our own world, but suddenly that seemed as if it might work against us. I kept my mouth shut.

"Our solution is perfect," Ada said. She put her hand between Toby's ears and scratched. "What do dogs do but lay around all day anyway? You could keep him as fat and lazy and silly as you want."

"That will simply never happen," Jessica said. "We will never be able to convince all of the people. In fact we will be able to convince very few. If you throw Holly off the bridge again, you could cause a war in here. I want you to think carefully. It won't be nice if there is artillery shelling going on in your mother's lungs. Hand-to-hand combat in her stomach. Swordplay in her heart. There will be cell damage. We are fighting for our very world. Would you destroy an entire people, an entire world, for your Mother?"

"Yes," Ada said at once.

I was glad I didn't have to answer that one. I didn't even want to think about it.

"And what will you do, Ada, if you force our society into a state of primitive savagery," Jessica said. "How do you think Holly will like having little bands of hunter/gatherers roaming around in her liver?"

"If her mind is free, she'll be able to handle her liver."

"We won't move to a dog," Jessica said, and then she was quiet.

Ada took her feet. "One more time, Barry."

"But what about all those people?" I asked.

"Shut up." Ada dropped Mom's feet and wiped tears from her own eyes with a big blue-checked handkerchief from her back pocket. I shut up and took Mom under the arms again.

We threw her over the side. Jessica didn't even scream this time.

We pulled her up after only a few bounces. Ada looked grim, and I feared that this whole business would fail. All those people. I could be honest with myself, at least in little short bursts. I understood how entire lives could be lived in minutes. I knew that Jessica was right when she said the nanopeople were as real as me. I understood that some of them were dying. We rolled Mom over. She looked dead herself, but when I grabbed her wrist, I felt a pulse. Ada sat her up and gently slapped her face over and over again. I scooted back and grabbed a soda out of the picnic basket and poured a little in my hand and flicked it at Mom. No response. Toby pushed his way in between Ada and me and licked Mom's face again.

Some time passed.

Then Jessica opened Mom's eyes.

"So much has changed." Jessica sounded weak, diminished somehow.

"But one thing is still firm. We will not abandon our world."

Ada sighed. I hoped she wouldn't want to toss Mom over the side again.

"We propose a compromise," Jessica said.

"We're listening," Ada said.

"We propose to let Holly have more control over her life," Jessica said. "We have combed through her memory and found a set of activities that we feel prepared to tolerate. Ballroom dancing, for example."

Ada's face got absolutely purple. Her hands closed in fists and opened in claws, closed and opened. When she spoke her voice was steady and cold but coiled like a spring, cobra tight. "You're telling me that you will allow Dr. Holly Ketchum, a respected physicist and leading authority on nanotechnology, a woman so full of curiosity and life that some people simply have to step out of her light or get burned, a woman vibrating with sexual vitality and gentle innocent love and openness for almost everyone—" She jumped up and shouted, "A woman who thrives on the adrenaline rush of white water and rock faces and free fall— you're telling me you're going to allow this woman to do ballroom dancing? Is that what you're telling me?"

"Well, yes. Among other things."

"Ada." I grabbed her hand, and the look she turned down on me would have loosened the bowels of a biker. "Let me try," I said. I thought she was going to say something to make me feel small or even hit me, but she jerked her hand away and stomped off to her truck instead. Toby and I watched as she kicked big dents in the door of her truck. When she stopped yelling and slumped to the ground, I turned to Mom and spoke to Jessica.

"If there is to be a compromise, Jessica," I said. "It will have to be on our terms. Or if you think about that a little, it'll have to be on

Mom's terms. You're going to have to learn to live with what your world wants, not what you want for your world."

"Well, we did come up with this list."

"You're going to have to let Mom come out and tell you want she wants."

"But she takes such chances!"

"You'll just have to learn to trust her," I said.

Jessica didn't reply, and I was suddenly at a loss. It seemed clear what must happen next, but I didn't know how to convince the nanopeople. I felt a hand on my shoulder and jerked my head around in time to see Ada squat down beside me.

"Barry's right," Ada said. "You must turn inward. You must let Mom take care of the stuff outside. You don't have what it takes to deal with things out here. We can keep throwing you off the bridge until your society is completely disrupted. If it starts to look like those of you who are left are getting used to bungee jumping, we can do something else. Access Mom's memory of alligator wrestling."

Jessica squinted Mom's eyes for a moment then jerked her head to the right as if Ada had slapped her.

"Look at ultra-light stunt flying," I said, encouraged again by Ada's support.

Jessica jerked Mom's head to the left.

"Do we need to go on?" Ada asked. "We won't quit."

Jessica let Mom's shoulders slump. She sighed. "We'll try it your way," she said. "We'll try it. But strictly on a trial basis!"

"No conditions," Ada said.

Jessica rolled Mom's eyes for a long time, then she said, "You win."

A smile grew on Mom's face, bigger and bigger, until she laughed out loud. "Ada! Barry!" She struggled with the ropes around her wrists. "I knew I could count on you two."

I could see it was Mom, something about the way the body was controlled convinced me Mom was to some degree in charge, but how much Mom was it? I worried that the nanopeople would have her on a short leash.

Toby lunged across my lap to get at her. The entire back end of his body wagged as he licked her face, and he could not contain his joy to the point that he peed all over me. I didn't know how Ada felt about it, but a Mom real enough to make a dog pee was a Mom real enough for me. I leaned in and kissed her cheek.

"Untie me," Mom said, twisting her head this way and that to avoid Toby's tongue.

Ada pushed the dog away and pulled the big blade from the sheath on her belt. She turned Mom around and cut her wrists loose.

Mom's hair turned brown even as she stripped off her sweater. Her eyes cleared; her skin tightened. She pulled the dreary housedress from first one shoulder and then the other and wiggled it down to her hips. She bounced a little and pulled the dress along with her under-wear down her thighs and over her knees. Ada undid the bungee boots and pulled them off Mom's feet. Mom's wrinkles disappeared and her bones straightened. When she stood, nude and magnificent and beaming a big smile at us, she was Mom in body again. Well, in a way. This was Mom, I thought, as she must have looked at thirty or so. Long reddish brown hair falling over slightly freckled shoulders. Pale blue eyes. Small high breasts. Long strong legs.

"Shall we go home, Mother?" Ada asked.

"Not so fast." Mom sat down on the bridge and pulled the bungee boots on again. "I need to pin down just who's boss in here." She climbed up on the bridge rail, and with a wild scream of joy did a perfect swan dive into the abyss.

We watched the arch of her dive and listened to her yell and watched her bounce.

"Do you suppose we've just postponed things?" I asked.

"What do you mean?"

"Well, what do you think will happen to her when we've either got nanopeople of our own or we've died? How about then?"

Ada seemed to think about that as we listened to Mom whoop at the upswing of each bounce.

"Well, maybe we'd better pull her up and get some motherly advice," Ada said.

No Comet

Convinced that my slant on Bohr's version of the Copenhagen interpretation of quantum mechanics was our last hope, I bullied Jane, who didn't want to be married to me anymore, and Sacha into cooperating with a final desperate attempt to save the world.

"This is stupid, Tim," Jane said, her voice softened a little by the brown paper bag over her head.

"La la, la la, la la," Sacha sang. She banged the heels of her shoes against the legs of her chair in time to her tune. Wearing a bag over her head was still fun, I thought, but our daughter was seven and had fidgeting down to a fine art. How long would she stick with me?

I'd pushed away my plate, but there was a sticky spot, orange marmalade probably, where I would have liked to put my hands. I put them in my lap instead. Breakfast had been tense. Jane had banged some pots around, scorched some eggs, burned some toast, warmed some bacon. I wished I'd brushed my teeth before I put a bag over my own head.

Everything was tan, but not an even tan; I imagined it was like looking through the dry, mottled skin of some desert creature, maybe a horned toad. There was a seam where the brown paper overlapped and joined to make a bag, and I couldn't see much light through that double layer. If I tilted my head back carefully, I could see what looked like the letter H in some fancy font (except for the way the seam came up and touched the cross piece of the H) made from the overlaps needed to square off and seal the bottom of the bag.

"I don't think I could have missed the fact that a comet is about to hit the Earth, Tim," Jane said.

"Do you read the newspapers?"

"No."

"Do you watch TV?"

"You know I don't."

"How about the radio?"

"Well, no. Not today."

"None of your goofy friends do either." I nailed down my point. "So just how do you think you would have heard about it?"

"That tone is exactly why I say we need to live apart, Tim."

"Boop boop boop be doop," Sacha sang.

"Everyone just relax," I said. "And keep your bags on." Things were slipping away. I needed to circle our wagons. It was vital that none of us give the world outside even a fleeting glance.

My own breath aside, the smell inside my bag reminded me of all the things you can carry in a brown paper bag. Curiously, the first thing that came to mind was books. Surely I'd carried home more groceries in brown paper bags than books. In fact, the name of the grocery store was printed right on the bag in red letters. Nevertheless, I thought of books, and clothes, and moving. I thought of garbage in the bags before I thought of groceries. Maybe it was because groceries spend so little time in the bags. I knew that if I packed my stuff up in paper bags, the bags might just sit for months in some cold new place.

"This isn't just my plan, Jane," I said. "The president has been on TV urging people not to look. Forests have been lighted to smoke up the skies. Teams are everywhere in primitive areas making sure no one looks."

"Even if there is a giant comet about to hit the Earth, just what good do you expect these bags to do?" Jane asked.

"Things that might happen can't be separated from the devices you use to measure them," I said. "You can't look at something without changing it."

"What?"

"The moon's not there if no one is looking. Or in our case, the comet."

"Like the tree in the forest?"

"Sort of," I said. "But that was philosophy. This is science."

"Oh, right. Sure."

"I have to go to the bathroom," Sacha said.

"Soon, honey," I said. "Just hang on a little while longer."

"Someone would peek," Jane said.

"Maybe. But it won't be us."

"How can that matter?"

"This is the same argument you use for not voting, Jane." I knew I should be soothing her instead of snapping at her, but I couldn't help it. "It's irresponsible. If everyone thought like you, no one would vote."

"Who's talking about voting? We're sitting around the kitchen table with grocery sacks over our heads!"

Sacha giggled.

I decided to try silence on Jane. I could hear my own breathing against the sides of the bag, and with any little movement there was a rustle like dry autumn leaves in a green plastic trash sack. I could hear birds too. They would be in the feeder outside the window over the sink. They would fly away if they caught us looking at them.

I could pull the bag away from my face a little and look straight down and see my white shirt over the gut hanging into my lap. I could suck the gut in; I could sigh it out. I could see my tan slacks, my black loafers, and the black and white kitchen tiles.

Strange, but I couldn't see the name of our grocery store through the bag. Had I put the bag on backwards? I twisted it around. I still couldn't see the letters, and then I didn't know which way the bag was. Were the red letters to the front or to the back? I felt unhooked, disoriented, lost.

Things suddenly got brighter. It is my opinion that that was when the comet touched the atmosphere, and because it didn't hit just then, I think the last person on Earth quit looking at it at precisely that moment.

"Don't you see the sudden light of the fire?"

"A cloud probably just moved away from the sun," Jane said.

I thought I heard some uncertainty in her voice. "That's what you'd like to think," I said.

"How long are we going to play this game, Tim?"

How long? Why, just until the comet's gone, I almost said. It hit me then that Jane's question was a good one. If finally no one was looking at the comet, did that mean it went away, or did it mean the comet was hanging frozen just inside the atmosphere, filling the entire sky, ready to plunge down on us as soon as we looked? Didn't that mean we could never look? Didn't that mean we were doomed to sit there at the kitchen table with bags over our heads forever?

"It makes no sense," Jane said. "What about intelligences on other planets? What if some alien shaman is looking at your comet through a telescope?"

"One of your saucer people?"

"At least there's good evidence for them. Unlike your stupid comet."

"Jane," I said, "if you looked out the window right now you'd see the sky filled with fire, and just because you looked, the comet would crash down and blow us all up."

"You're scaring me, Daddy," Sacha said.

"Don't worry, honey." I would have liked to touch her hand, but I couldn't reach her. "Nothing can hurt you if you keep your head in the bag."

"You're teaching her to be an ostrich!"

"What's an ostrich?" Sacha asked.

"Is that why you won't let me have the weekends?" I asked.

"Yes."

"I really, really have to go, Daddy," Sacha said.

I heard them shifting in their chairs, moving around, trying to be quiet, but not succeeding. I heard them whispering. Fear turned me to stone. The game was up. I pictured Jane quietly slipping off her bag and setting it aside, pictured her carefully removing Sacha's bag, saw Jane grin and roll her eyes in my direction and put her finger to her lips so Sacha would be quiet, saw them both looking at me stiff in my bag, the two of them, the little alien, the Russian girl, our surprising blond Sacha, and the big one, looking so sweetly sad suddenly, Jane. It wasn't that she hated me, I realized. She'd moved on when I wasn't looking. She was bored, restless; we had so little in common these days. She wandered like a wounded bird, one leg missing maybe, circling east, and I plodded ever westward. What in the world did we have to talk about?

I saw Sacha make an O of her mouth when she looked at the window and saw the comet peeking in at us like an angry red eye filling the sky. I saw the comet leap to Earth and fire the trees, the city, our house. Burning hurricane winds knocked down our walls and crisped our skin and peeled our bones.

I cried out.

Jane snatched the bag from my head.

Sunshine turned the refrigerator into a gleaming white block, an alien monolith that had popped into existence among our chrome pots and wooden bowls. From somewhere far away came the tiny tinkle tinkle of an ice-cream truck. I looked at the window over the sink, and in a flutter of squawks and black wings, birds fled the feeder.

"It's easy to see what happened," I said. "You were right, Jane. Someone peeked. But we didn't. And because we didn't, by the time we looked, we'd split off into a reality in which the comet never existed in the first place. We're saved!"

"Oh, Daddy." Sacha hugged me quickly, then ran off to the bathroom.

"Okay," Jane said, "you can have every other weekend. But we take the cat."

"What cat?" I asked.

THERE IS DANGER

There is danger in regarding her as a goddess, danger in speculating about the lazy smile she directs at me over the Dover sole, the lemony finger bowls, the steaming rice, and bright green spears of asparagus, her gray eyes dancing with golden candlelight, danger in the provocative tilt of her head, her long chestnut hair flowing over her bare shoulder.

Selena reaches over the table and traces her fingertips softly over my hand. My hair bursts into flames. I know she notices, but she chooses not to comment. Our waiter runs over and pours a pitcher of ice water over my head.

My ears will be red. I'll have to wear a big bandage, like a white turban, to work tomorrow. The women will arch their eyebrows at me. Most of the men will pretend not to notice. Ed Cory in the office next door will come over and give me a shot to the ribs with his elbow and say, "I can see you've been out with Selena again." I'll tell him I may be getting too old for this. After all, I'll say, the Boogie Woogie Bugle Boy could have been my older brother.

I wave our waiter away, assuring him that I really am A-OK. Really. It's nothing. Selena picks at her fish.

"It was wonderful at the beach today," I say.

Our grandchildren played together. My little Amy sat in the sand not so much timid as awestruck, her mouth a little O, blue eyes wide, staring up at Selena's Bradley who stood over her with his hands on his hips, his stomach pouching out over his diaper like he'd already discovered the joys and sorrows of beer. The waves came in, the waves went out, but the children only had eyes for one another. I watched Selena rise from the ocean like Aphrodite (but there is danger in that thought), shaking the water from her long, slender body, then running easily up the beach to us, seagulls marking her time with their cries. There was sand tangled in the hair at the back of my thighs. My chest felt warm. Selena dropped down beside us and dug into the big wicker picnic basket. Amy rolled over in the sand to watch, and I grabbed her and lifted her into the air then plunged her down to growl into her stomach. She giggled and slapped at my ears. Bradley put grape soda fingers on my shoulder and looked up at me with his deep brown eyes, so I grabbed him too, and growled into his stomach. When I put the children down, they scampered to Selena. She gave them each a sandwich. The sandwiches looked as big as hardbound books in their small hands. Children know it; they know where to go; men are not nurturing.

"Wasn't it, though?" she says. "I hope the children didn't get too much sun."

We finish our fish.

"Let's dance," Selena says. She knows I dance mechanically but will do almost anything to touch her. We go onto the floor. The music tries to chase me around like a garden hose after a dirty dog, but I won't let it. I take a small shuffle step to the right and point with both hands to the left (little six-shooters), then I take a small shuffle step to the left and point to the right. This is the way I do these modern dances.

Selena rocks; she rolls; she remembers Woodstock. Her hair flies around her face. Her skirt swirls, dipping between her thighs. She never takes her eyes off mine.

I point. I shoot. It's all in the thumbs.

The music stops then starts again, slow saxophones, brushes on the drums this time, and Selena whirls into my arms. Her warmth staggers me. I feel dizzy.

"You're trembling," she whispers in my ear, her breath shooting laser light through my head.

"I know."

"What are you thinking?"

She wants to know what I'm feeling, but she doesn't want to be unpleasantly surprised. I don't know what to tell her. Men are not open. We have ages of practice in not saying it; we've got it down pat. We are bull elephants, footloose and free in the forest and the grasslands, apart and aloof but endlessly irritating, sniping at the edges of the herd of females and calves, trunk slapping each other on the ass, saying, what a shot, man, and how's the market this morning, and the best leaves are on the jujube trees, and way to go, Key Moe Sobby! We're bears, sufficient unto ourselves, always chased away afterwards in case we are seized by an urge to eat the children. We're snakes and, like her goldfish, we have no use for bicycles. Pigs. Oink, my man, you getting any lately, and what you got under that hood, and how about those Lakers?

Selena nips at the lobe of my ear with her teeth. My left foot gives way, and I stumble forward out of her arms and fall to my knees.

She pulls me up and helps me back to the table and kneels before me and removes my shoe and sock. I pull my foot into my lap and see that the bones of my toes are missing. My toes hang like limp pale pink balloons at the end of my foot. I touch my big toe with a first finger and thumb; it feels soft and silky, but empty, the nail a hard imperfection that I'm tempted to scratch off. I flip my dangling toes with my fingers and they swing back and forth. I put my sock and shoe back on.

"You'll have to let me lean on you when we leave," I say.

Her grin makes me want to howl at the moon.

"Okay, you can lean on me," she says.

Our waiter comes round with the desert cart. Selena selects a chocolate mousse. I go with the cheesecake.

"Tell me something astonishing," she says. I notice there is a smudge of chocolate at the corner of her mouth. Her tongue flashes, licks it off, and I miss my cheesecake and clang my fork loudly against my plate.

"Well?" she says.

I open my mouth to speak, and my tongue shoots out, long and thin and stiff like a wooden tongue depressor, and the squatting figure of my father on the end of it opens his mouth to speak, and his tongue shoots out and on the end of it the hunched form of my grandfather opens his mouth to speak, and his tongue shoots out and on the end of it the knotty form of my great-grandfather opens his mouth to speak, and on and on, until from somewhere deep in my primordial past, a small, lonely voice says, "I love you, Selena."

"What?"

I put cheesecake in my mouth and smile around it. Men are not romantic; we don't have much to say. Maybe we really have no deep feelings. We cannot wait to get out of our pants. We see only body parts, we think only of conquests, we never want to stay the whole night. We've got things to do.

Our waiter puts a little black lacquered tray with the check on our table.

We fence with our gold cards for a few minutes, finally agreeing that since she paid for the picnic this afternoon, I can pick up the check for dinner. I ask our waiter to pour us some coffee and call us a cab.

Selena drinks her coffee and nods her head from side to side in time to the music. I drum my fingers on the table.

Before I know it, our waiter is tapping me on the shoulder, whispering our cab is waiting. I push myself up from the table. Selena comes around and offers me her shoulder to lean on. I put my arm around her, and she looks up at me.

"You okay?"

I have to swallow hard; there is danger I could fall into those eyes, fall and fall forever. I nod, and she steps forward. I know I'm too heavy.

The hostess in her bright white blouse and black skirt tells us to have a nice day as we make our way around the potted plants and into the street. The driver is holding the back door of his cab open for us.

On the way to her place, Selena leans her head against the glass of the back window and gazes out at the bright city rushing by. I watch her hand resting palm up on her knee. I would probably fall on my face if I were to lean forward and touch my lips to her fingers.

We don't speak.

The cab driver takes her money then helps me to her door and supports me, my left arm around his shoulder, while I lean in close to Selena. She's got her back to the door, and her eyes shine in the moonlight. I ignore the driver's stubbly face at my shoulder like a second head and kiss her.

The rest of my bones disappear, and I slip down her body, slip out of the driver's grip, like an eel socked between the eyes. The driver catches me by my belt in the back.

I hang bent double, unable to see her face.

"Well, I guess I'd better be going," I say.

The driver walks back toward the cab, carrying me like a suitcase. His boots crunch the gravel of her driveway. Crickets sing, and a warm honeysuckle breeze strokes my face. Between my limp and dangling legs, I can see Selena standing on her stoop, a halo of moonlight in her hair. She raises a hand to wave.

"I had a wonderful time," she calls, filling me with delicious joy.

"I'll call you!" I shout.

I'll send her roses. I'll write her a poem. My secret is not so much in knowing what women want; men can never know that. My secret is knowing what they'll settle for. Even so, there is danger.

PINK SMOKE

Maggie liked to steal things. Only a few days into their relationship, she stole a candy bar and slipped it into Joe's shirt pocket as they left the mini-mart. He found it before they got to the car, and he wanted to give it back.

"You better not," she told him.

He didn't listen.

The guy in the mini-mart looked mean and dangerous, and Joe was suddenly sure he had a gun under the counter.

"You're saying you want a refund?" the guy asked. "I can't give you a refund. How do I know what you did with that candy bar?"

"No, I don't want a refund," Joe said. "I just want to give it back to you."

"You want to give me your candy bar? How do I know you didn't use a needle to inject poison into that candy bar? You go ahead and get out of here now."

"Look," Joe said, "I didn't pay for this candy bar, so I can't take it."

"What do you mean you didn't pay for it?" the guy said. "You mean you stole it?"

"No."

"I think maybe you better freeze right there while I call the cops."

Joe ran out of the mini-mart. Maggie was behind the wheel of his car. He didn't know how she had gotten it started. He jumped into the shotgun seat, and she threw the car into gear and they sped away.

"Hey, nice going," she said a little later. "You pulled it off."

"What are you talking about?" He was still having some trouble getting his breathing under control.

She grinned at him and looked down at his hand. He followed her gaze and saw that he still clutched the candy bar. It was a crushed mess now, but stolen nonetheless. Loot.

"How did you get the car started?" he asked.

"I used the key," she said.

He looked, and yes, there was the key in the ignition. He leaned up on one hip and pushed his hand into the front pocket of his jeans, and no, his keys weren't there.

She had picked his pocket.

Maggie had been a magician's assistant in another life. She was never very definite as to when that other life had been, or where. A long time ago. Somewhere back east. She'd learned a lot of tricks. She could take the watch right off your wrist justlikethat and leave you none the wiser. She liked to pull things out of Joe's ears in public—coins, cheeses, once a bunch of broccoli.

He sometimes thought she might be more trouble than she was worth. Maybe he'd move on. Maybe next week. Maggie claimed to be 36. Joe was 41. There was still time for a nasty breakup, years of painful therapy, slow healing, and then someday someone else. The next woman in his life might be a fighter pilot or a taxidermist. He really wasn't in over his head with Maggie. And there was that stealing business.

"Hey, look," she said when he opened the door. "I brought the wine." She held up a couple of bottles of wine—one red, one white, both too big to be plausibly hidden on her person. Maybe she'd swiped them one at a time? No, she would have done them both at once. She could be so distracting. Tonight she wore an incredibly colorful T-shirt with target swirls of red and green and blue that pulled the eye in toward her breasts and then away up and over her shoulders and back again just in time to be blinded by a smile. Cut-off jeans, which meant she could put one leg out and snatch your attention (was this when she planted the produce in his ears?). Sandals. And every toenail a different color. If you looked very closely, and you wanted to look very closely, you might notice there were messages in tiny letters written on her toenails like bumper stickers—if you can read this you're too close!

She held the wine out away from her body with both hands and stepped up on her toes and kissed him on the cheek. When he opened his eyes, he had to take a step forward so he wouldn't stumble into the hallway. She had slipped by him.

After dinner, he lighted a fire and they settled on the couch with coffee. He put his arm around her shoulders and pulled her close, and she sighed and snuggled in. She idly moved one hand up and down the front of his shirt, expertly unfastening and fastening the buttons. He thought she was not even aware that she was doing it, until he felt her cool hand on his chest. He kissed her. He could feel her muscles moving under his hands, as if he were holding a cat when it doesn't want to be held, but Maggie wanted to be held. He was lost in the kiss and the feel of her, the smell of her. There was something else happening just under the surface. He imagined opening his eyes and seeing that the scene had changed, that they were no longer on his couch in front of the fire, but had been moved magically to a South Seas beach. He could almost feel the wind moving across the bare skin of his back.

85

Then with a cheerful "Ta da!" Maggie leaped away from him, and as she went, she took his shirt, his pants, his shorts, his shoes and socks, his watch. He flopped back onto the cushions stunned and completely naked.

"I think it's just so incredibly sexy, me being fully dressed with a naked man," she said. "Don't you?"

He did.

The night she stood him up, he figured it had finally ended. He'd been waiting for the other shoe to drop. And this was it. He knew that he made most of his own problems with such thinking, but he couldn't help it with Maggie. Maybe it was because he never had understood why she would have been interested in him in the first place.

He drank a little too much that evening and went to bed early. When the phone rang at three in the morning, it took him a long time to rub the stupidity out of his eyes and ears.

Maggie was in jail.

So, she hadn't stood him up after all.

"That's a heck of an excuse," he said.

"What are you talking about?" she said. "Come on, Joe, wake up. Can you help me out here? I know it's asking a lot."

"I'll be there." He didn't know where the jail was. She gave him precise directions.

She'd been busted for shoplifting—captured on video, a stupid lapse on her part, she told him. That was bad enough. But she'd also drawn a cop she couldn't charm. He wasn't the least bit amused when she returned his handcuffs with a smile after he'd locked her hands behind her back. Joe wondered if she'd said "Ta da!" He bet she had. The cop had called for backup and, before she knew it, there were so many grim-faced men and women in uniform, you might have thought she'd knocked over a bank, and taken a dozen hostages.

Joe took her back to his place. He wanted to yell at her. He didn't. He wanted to ask her how she could be so stupid. She didn't have to steal things. It wasn't like she was starving. He didn't say that either. He made her tea while she used his shower. She came out of the bathroom dressed in his red robe, her hair wrapped up in a towel, and they sat at the kitchen table and drank tea and didn't talk much. Later he tucked her into his bed and sat for a while watching her sleep.

Maggie was so angry, she was vibrating and humming like a robot about to explode and splatter machine parts all over the landscape. The two of them were stomping down the street and people were getting out of their way.

"You've got to go back to your shrink," Joe said.

"I won't."

"They'll send you back to jail."

"Let them. I'll bust out."

"Then they'll just shoot you, Maggie."

"Good!"

She snatched the hat off a passing woman and pushed it into Joe's hands. The woman didn't notice.

"Hey!" Joe said. He stopped, but Maggie kept moving. He hurried to catch up with her.

She took a watch from a passing man and gave it to him. She bumped another man, said oh excuse me, and then gave Joe the man's wallet. They hadn't stopped moving. Maggie grabbed a purse and pushed it into his arms. He was carrying a lot of stuff now. All they needed was for someone to notice and start yelling for the cops and he'd be standing there with his arms full of stolen goods.

"Maggie, for Christ sakes stop this."

She shot a hand into a man's coat, did a little dance with him that left him looking dazed, and then handed Joe the man's tie and shirt and kept walking.

They passed a hot dog cart and she gave Joe a jumbo frank with sauerkraut and they kept walking. She snatched the glasses off a bald man and the pearls from a woman with a cane.

"Stop it, Maggie!" Joe yelled.

"What do you want from me?" Maggie said, still so angry there should have been smoke billowing from her ears. "I didn't take her cane. And you know I could have."

They rushed by a man on a bench reading a newspaper. Maggie snatched out the sports section and slapped it onto the pile of stuff Joe carried.

In the distance, sirens screamed and he was sure they screamed for him. He stopped dead in his tracks. "I can't go on like this, Maggie," he called after her.

She looked over her shoulder and said, "So stay where you are!" After she'd turned the corner, but before the patrol car flashed onto the scene, Joe deposited the things she had stolen from the pedestrians into a trash barrel. He turned the other way and tried to blend in with the crowd.

Joe lost track of Maggie while she was doing time. He had written her often in the beginning, and she had always answered—funny letters. You'd think from reading her letters she was having a great time in jail. He wasn't fooled.

She'd served about half her 18 months when her letters stopped. He called the jail. Was he family? Well, not exactly. They wouldn't tell him anything. He kept writing for another month. Then he stopped. He was pretty sure he would have heard if she'd died in jail. It wasn't like they lived in such a harsh place you could die in jail and not be mentioned in the daily papers.

He liked to think she was getting help. Maybe in jail they'd make her see a doctor who could figure out why she had to steal things. Maybe she would change. Maybe she already had. Maybe she'd gotten to a place in her life where a guy like Joe just didn't make sense any more.

The month of her release came and went. He hadn't been sure of the exact date anyway. He couldn't just hang around the jail waiting for her to come out. He did hang around waiting for her to call. She didn't call.

The next woman in Joe's life was a freelance creator of computer games. Her name was Roberta. She was all the time shooting him with imaginary ray guns. She had a ten-year-old daughter named Tiffany and a sixteen-year-old son named Sam. One night Sam tried to strangle Joe with the cable that hooked his mother's computer to the laser printer. Joe decided he wasn't cut out to be a dad. He and Roberta weren't together anymore.

There were posters all over town.

The Amazing Maggie! Come one, come all. See her pull a rabbit out of a hat. See her pull a hat out of a rabbit. Put her in a box and watch her get out of it! You won't believe your eyes.

The big question for Joe was whether he wanted to be in the first row or not.

Opening night, Joe took a seat somewhere in the middle of the third row—not too near, not too far. When the lights went down, he decided he had agonized for nothing. She probably couldn't see him anyway.

The curtain went up. The band jumped into a song, long and lazy in the beginning so the dancing men in black tie, tails, and top hats could tap along with their walking sticks, picking up the pace, putting on the Ritz, lining up along the stage, and then in the middle pulling back into a big V so Maggie could appear in a thundering explosion of pink smoke.

Ta da!

Nobody's assistant now, she was the main event, a headliner. She did card tricks. She made things appear and disappear. She made things float in the air. She was really very good.

So, did she look either sadder or wiser? Joe couldn't tell. Mostly she just looked good. She seemed totally at ease on stage. She loved the audience and the audience loved her back.

Could he take credit for any of it? Probably not. At best, he'd been practice for her, and there had been jail and therapy and whatever else she'd been up to since he'd lost track of her.

She lined up her dancing men and pulled produce from their ears. Cantaloupes! Watermelons! Fat zucchinis.

Hey, no fair, Joe thought, that's our trick!

"For this next part," she said, and from the shadows came a drum roll, "I need a volunteer from the audience."

A spotlight swept across the crowd, and when it passed him, he thought he saw her eyes widen a little.

Okay. Now or never again. Joe jumped to his feet.

"Me," he shouted, "pick me!"

SEASON FINALE

I am a P.I. on TV. You'd know me if you saw me. Sam, who is the brother of my dead lover, knows me. He grabs my arm as I step out of Brinkmann's Hollywood Pharmacy.

"You!" he says. I can see the emotions swashbuckling on his face. He's purple with anger, but he's got this goofy grin that keeps going off and on like he can't believe his luck. Being bald and beefy with tattoos on his hairy arms, he doesn't look much like Pamela.

"Hello, Sam," I say. "How are you holding up?" I expect him to ask me if I found out who killed Pamela.

He punches me in the mouth.

I fall to the sidewalk, and he comes down on my chest, pinning my arm with his knees. He pummels my face with his fists. People step around us.

"Help!" I call, but no one comes to my aid. No doubt they think we're filming. My lights go out.

It's not a pretty sight I see when next I'm able to open my swollen eyes. Pam's mom is stirring something on the stove, and a long ash

91

from the cigarette in her mouth falls into the pot. Pam's dad folds his newspaper and gives me the eye. Sam is punching his left palm with his right fist. I want to touch my face but find that I'm tied to my chair. Pam herself is across the table from me, and she looks cold and blue. There are crystals in her honey hair, and a little icicle hangs from her nose. She sits at attention.

"Let's begin, Mother," Pam's dad says.

I can see that this is going to be bad.

Pam had died off-stage. I had imagined her going peacefully—a sweet, gentle drifting away on puffy clouds of poison. I can see now that that isn't true. Her face is a frozen scream.

"I vote guilty." Pam's mom taps her spoon on the edge of the pot. She throws her cigarette in the sink then produces another, like magic, from the apron bulging over her belly.

"Me too," says Sam, still punching one hand into the other.

"Whoa now! Hold on," says Pam's dad. "Let's hear what Pammy's got to say." He looks at her, then he looks at me. "Doesn't she look nice? We've been keeping her cold for you. What? What's that you say, Pammy?" He leans his head close to Pam's gaping mouth. "She says she loved you, Mr. Nasal Spray. She says you could always make her laugh." He twists head around until both he and Pam are staring at me, and he laughs that squeaky laugh of hers: hee, hee, hee. He's got it down just right.

Then his face gets mean. "She says you killed her, Mr. Mouth Wash."

I can see that I'm in some trouble here.

"Why would I do that? We were going to be married!" Didn't they understand that the girl always dies once the hero decides to marry her? It's sad, but that's the way things are. It's an absolute law of the universe: when the TV hero loves, the beloved dies. I can't help it. Can I flap my arms and fly?

"Pammy says guilty, and I say guilty." Pam's dad puts his hands on the table and pushes himself to his feet. "So that makes it unanimous."

Sam drags my chair away from the table and jerks me upright.

"Hey!" I say. "Hey, wait! I was in the studio at the time."

"The studio?" Pam's dad looks puzzled.

"At the time?" Pam's mom smiles a shrewd smile.

"My show, you know?" I try again.

Sam belts me a good one in the stomach. "What show? You work in a goddamn drug store!"

"That's just my cover!" I probably shouldn't have told them that, but what with the way I was struggling to get my breath after Sam punched me, they may not have understood the significance of my remark anyway.

Pam's dad picks her up. She's still sitting at attention, and he looks like a man moving furniture.

They drag me off to the cellar.

Sam padlocks one end of a chain around my neck. The other end is welded to a metal ring on the wall. He cuts my arms free, and, still wobbly from all the excitement, I sit on the stone floor. Pam's dad puts her in a chair facing me.

"She may seem cold now," Pam's dad says. "But she'll warm up to you." He knocks his knuckles against an oil drum by my side. I see that way down low there's a little silver faucet hooked to the drum. "Here's your water."

"You get to sit in your own shit." Sam grins at me.

"You can't say 'shit' on TV," I tell him.

Pam's mom leans down close. "Pammy told me all your stories, Mr. Feminine Hygiene Spray. We was like two girls, Pammy and me. Well, this is going to be close up and in color. In a few days my Pammy will be wearing her special perfume just for you, Mr. Speed Stick. She'll get that special look. Ain't no fade-away."

RAY VUKCEVICH

"Let's go, Mother," Pam's dad is on the stairs. "Hawaii's waiting. Come on, Sammy, you don't want to miss those hula girls."

They go away and leave me there with Pam. The door above bangs shut, making the light bulb on its long wire swing and the shadows dance. Pam just sits there looking at me. I can see that the icicle on her nose has melted.

"Okay, okay," I say.

It's not our ordinary stuff, and the writers will have a hell of time getting me out of this one. My fans will puzzle over it all summer. It'll drive them crazy.

"Fade to black," I say.

Nothing happens.

THE SWEATER

S
he had obviously made it herself, so what was there to do but to try it on?

"Okay, here goes," he said.

"Happy birthday to you," she sang softly. "Happy birthday to you."

The sweater felt a little scratchy. It was green with big red horizontally stretched diamonds.

"Happy birthday, dear Geoffrey."

It smelled like straw or maybe clean sheep eating straw. He pulled it over his head.

"Happy birthday to you!"

Inside it was a lot darker than he'd expected. Was the weave so tight no light at all could penetrate? The neck hole was tight around the top of his head. He tugged gently. He could imagine Alice sitting across the table looking at him. Smiling smiling smiling. She would be freeze-face-smiling so when his head popped out of the sweater hole ta da! there she'd be smiling smiling smiling saying oh I hope you like it and it looks so good on you. She'd be waiting for the million questions he must have.

He should use this time in the dark to come up with some questions. How long did you work on it? What is it made of? Where did you get the yarn? How come I never saw you knitting?

He had, of course, seen her knitting but that would not be something he should admit. He pulled a little harder. Had she misjudged the size of his head?

Alice would be looking at his brown hair poking out the sweater hole like an animal backing out of its den. Inside, in the dark, he sensed a vast and empty space.

"Hello," he said.

"What?"

"I'm just checking the echoes," he said.

"Echoes?"

He pulled hard and sat up straight and strained to poke his head through the neck hole of the sweater. No dice. If he pulled too hard the sweater might squeeze down his face, certainly wiping the smile if not the nose from his face. He might lose his face altogether and pop out as a skull with chattering teeth and a small patch of hair on top exactly the size of the neck hole.

He stopped struggling. It might be easier to roll the thing up so his arms would be on the outside and he could get more leverage, maybe do a screw-top routine, but that would mean he couldn't appear magically to meet her smile with one of his own. He stretched his arms out, groping in the darkness for the boundaries of this new place. There didn't seem to be any boundaries and now he couldn't even feel the rough wool against his face. He could feel the tight band of the hole around his head. It was a headache that swoops in like a pigeon to land on your head and after some speculative pecking, spreads its wings and hugs your head tight, quivering.

It reminded him of the infamous medieval hat torture and the dream of some guy in a black mask roasting a silver derby until it glowed red and then pushing it down onto Geoffrey's head where it sizzled and popped and he rolled over and Alice moaned in her sleep.

"Give me a flashlight," he said.

"What?"

"I need a flashlight," he said.

"Aren't you going to put on the sweater?"

"I'm trying to put on the sweater," he said, "but I can't see what I'm doing."

She was silent.

"Are you out there?" he asked.

She sighed, and then he heard her slide her chair back. Her steps across the kitchen floor. The junk drawer to the left of the dishwasher opening. Stuff rattling. Her steps back to the table. "Here," she said.

"You've got the flashlight?"

"Yes."

"Poke it up under the edge and let me have it," he said.

A moment later he felt cold metal against his stomach, and he groped down and grabbed the flashlight. It felt like a little man with a big head.

"Thanks," he said.

She didn't reply, but he could tell she was back in her chair across the table again.

He flipped on the flashlight.

The light was bright green, unearthly. It made his hands glow green, but it didn't reach the far wall. He turned in a circle but the light didn't reach any of the walls. He pointed it up. The ceiling was too high to see. He walked forward but got no closer to the wall, and then it hit him that since the walls were attached to the roof and the top of his head was lodged in a hole in the roof, as he moved, the

RAY VUKCEVICH

roof moved, and as the roof moved, the walls moved, so no matter
how quickly he walked he would never reach any of the walls.

There might well be secret doors in the walls. He might find them
if he could run his hands over the walls. If he could get close enough
to shine his green light on the walls, he might find hairline cracks
marking the secret doors. He could reach down into his pants pocket
and get his pocket knife and slide the blade into a hairline crack and
pry the door, open pass out of the darkness and into a meadow.
There would be trees and birds in the trees, and the trees would line a
gurgling creek with silvery blue fish darting about and looking up at
him nervously when he settled on the bank and put his feet in the
water.

He would never get his feet wet if he couldn't get to the wall and
the secret door. How far could the wall be? Maybe if he pulled his
head way back (bringing the wall closer) and stretched his arms way
out, he might be able to get his fingernails into the hairline crack of
the secret door. Best check the echo again.

"Hello," he said.

"Hello again," she said. "What are you doing in there?"

"Looking for a way out," he said.

"Here, let me help."

"Don't!"

Too late.

She seized the sweater on either side of his head and yanked down
with tremendous force. The roof collapsed over his head, but his nose
and ears stopped it before his head could be completely exposed. He
looked down the slope of the sweater and it was like the sides of
volcano that had just pushed his head out of the earth instead of a
bunch of lava. He looked across the table at Alice. She wasn't smiling.

"Work your arms up into the sleeves," she said.

"What about my nose and ears?" His voice was muffled.

"Me, me, me," she said.

"It *is* my birthday."

"Yes," she said. "You're right. I'm sorry."

He let go of the flashlight and it rolled off his lap and fell onto the floor.

"What was that?" she asked.

"The flashlight," he said.

She ducked under the table.

"You've broken off the little alien's head," she said from under the table.

"The flashlight had a little alien head?"

"Not anymore," she said.

He looked down the slope of the sweater and across the mesa cluttered with cups and saucers, salt and pepper, sugar and the bright remains of bows and box and paper that had contained his birthday gift. Her empty place. He waited for her to reappear, but she didn't come back up from under the table.

"What are you doing under there?" he asked.

"I'm walking under a slate-gray rainy sky," she said. "I can see the ocean in the distance. I'm just going to keep walking until I get there."

"Is there any gum stuck to the sky?"

"Scratches." she said. "Streaks and scratches. Little hills. It isn't easy to tell what's the ground and what's the sky."

He worked his hands out from beneath the sweater and rolled it up to his nose and worked it down his face. He got his arms in the sleeves.

"Come out," he said. "I've managed to get the sweater on."

No answer.

HOME REMEDY

Perry took another look at the things he'd laid out on the lid of the closed toilet, everything lined up precisely, like a tray of doctor tools: ice pick, pliers, and a spray can of ant-and-roach poison. This was going to hurt. Yes, it would hurt, but nothing else had worked. Nose drops just made them frisky.

Time was not on his side. He had to quiet things down in his nose before Carmela woke up and came rubbing her eyes and scratching her butt and knocking on the bathroom door. She didn't yet realize that he was the source of their infestation.

Perry picked up the red and green can of bug spray and took a moment to puzzle out the backwards letters when viewed in the mirror—black letters spelling bug death in reverse. Did that spell life for him then? Well, that was the question, wasn't it? He put the white nozzle of the bug spray to his left nostril, took a deep breath through his mouth, and pushed the button. Fire raged through his nose and into his head, burning down the forest behind his eyes, chasing crazy black and yellow dream birds into his sudden tears. He swallowed a scream. His nose bulged and contracted as something inside punched around, fighting to get out. He sneezed, sneezed again. The maddening tickle ceased on the left, and a slick brown roach, as long as the first two joints of his little finger, slid out of his nose.

As clear as day, a sudden picture in his head: Perry's ten and staying at his uncle's ranch in Arizona, and the cow in the pen behind the barn is giving birth on this winter morning, and the steaming calf, all bloody and brown and wet, just hangs there for a moment from the end of the cow before falling to the cold manure with a plop.

The roach slid over his upper lip and fell tumbling into the water-stained yellow bowl of his bathroom sink and landed on its back with its legs all folded up and moving weakly as if in prayer. Perry put the bottom edge of the ant-and-roach can on the bug and pushed. The roach folded up like a man doing a sit-up before the can cut it in half with a crunch. The top half flipped over and dragged itself to the drain and disappeared. He turned on the cold water and washed the bottom half down too.

Perry speculated briefly on the proposition that all things separated someday somehow come together again. Going around, coming around. Like the way when you threw your bowling ball, you always got it back. He could feel his heart beating in his face. He closed his eyes and tried to breathe through his nose. The right side was still stopped up absolutely, but he was able to get a weak stream of foul-smelling air in through the left. He didn't fool himself that he'd cleared everything out of there. He knew what roaches and their leavings smelled like, and that smell was still in his nose, in spite of the bug spray. He felt dizzy, and he grabbed onto the sink. The jolt that had stunned the roach had done its job on him too. He wondered if he dare do his right side.

"You in there, Perry?" Carmela called.

So she was up. Perry pulled himself together and picked up the ice pick. Maybe he could spear a few and avoid taking another shot of the bug spray. Maybe he could do it before he had to deal with Carmela. He put the point of the ice pick in his right nostril and slowly probed upwards. He felt the roaches scurry away from the sharp tool, pressing themselves tighter into his sinuses. The itch and tickle of their scrambling legs and questing antennae made him bite his lips and squint his eyes. He pushed a little more with the ice pick and felt it break into one of the hard shells. The activity in his nose became frantic, and behind him Carmela pounded on the door. Perry flinched and stabbed himself somewhere deep inside his right nostril.

"Come on, Perry. Open up. I gotta pee!" Carmela banged on the bathroom door again. It sounded like artillery shelling.

Blood flooded from Perry's nose. "Go away, you cow. I'm bleeding!"

"Who're you calling a cow!" Carmela yelled. She rattled the knob and kicked the door. "I'll show you a cow! Let me in!"

Perry threw the ice pick at the toilet. Too dangerous with Carmela distracting him every minute. He was lucky he hadn't lost an eye. Why couldn't she have slept a little longer? In fact, why did this whole mess have to be happening to him? What kind of world is it where bugs crawl up your nose but leave your crabby wife alone? A world where you're 37 and as bald as honeydew melon already; a world where you can't smoke, because you cough up your lungs when you do; where you can't eat red meat because your cholesterol is too high; a world where you can't take a drink because your daddy died of it and it makes your knees knock to think about being like that— although you have been, you really have been, just ask Carmela, but you don't want to think about that right now, after all, you've got bugs up your nose—a world where you've got a going-nowhere-fast job, Jesus, some young punk called you Pop on the dock just the other day; a world where your wife is fooling around with someone, you don't know who, but someone. That kind of world. Any more questions?

"Are you going to let me in?" Carmela banged on the door again. She was quiet a moment, then she said, "I'm going to pee in your precious bowling bag if you don't let me use the toilet, Perry."

He didn't say anything, but he hated the thought of her squatting like a skinny white frog over his genuine leather bowling bag doing her business. The guys had given him that bag last year after he took City mostly all by himself.

"I'm going now," she said, and he could hear her moving away from the door. "Here I go walking toward the closet to get your bowling bag, Perry. Can you hear me walking to get your bowling bag? Stomp, stomp, stomp. I'm at the closet. I'm opening the door. I'm picking up your bowling bag. Last chance, Perry."

Another of life's never-ending irritations, Perry thought. He could wash his ball, but he'd never get the smell out of his bag. He took his finger away from his right nostril and blood streamed into the sink. Suddenly angry at the entire universe, Perry snatched up the bug poison and gave his right nostril a good long spray. To hell with caution.

"I'm peeing in your bowling bag, Perry!"

Perry's nose jumped around on his face like it wanted to get off. It felt like the residents in there had decided to get out of town but had forgotten the way and were just busting down the walls, cutting corners, going cross-country. He felt them tumbling down into the top of his throat, and he gagged and spit bugs into the sink. They landed, lively, and scrambled over the edge and dropped to the floor and dashed under the door.

"Squirt, squirt. Pee, pee," Carmela yelled. "Can you hear me peeing in your bowling bag, Perry?"

The pain in Perry's head was like being slapped hard on both ears at the same time by a big TV wrestler, and he slumped to the floor still holding onto the sink with one hand. He squeezed his eyes shut.

Another head picture: Perry's in bed on his back staring at a ceiling he can't see because it's absolutely dark in the bedroom; he can't see his hand in front of his face; in fact, he moves his hand up in front of his face to check that; right, he can't see it, but he can feel the roaches leaving his nose. He struggles not to scream and jump up clawing at his face. They come out at night, and the reason Carmela knows about them is that they don't all come crawling back to his nose in the morning. Some of them stay out and breed and live in the kitchen cabinets and in her underwear drawers and behind the couch and in the bathtub and beneath the sink—everywhere. It's not so astonishing, he thinks, that a kind of roach has developed that can live in his nose. After all, they live almost everywhere else. He read once about a roach that lives in TVs and never comes out until the TV dies. The bugs in TV-land listen to the programs and the commercials and eat the insulated guts of their machines. Snug. It's not so surprising that a cousin would get around to Perry's nose sooner or later.

Perry opened his eyes. He snatched up the bug spray. If, when he sprayed his nose, they exited his mouth, it stood to reason that if he sprayed his mouth they'd exit his nose. So he opened wide and sprayed, realizing almost at once that his logic was flawed. His stomach twisted, and he had only time to throw open the lid of the toilet before throwing up in the bowl.

"I hear what you're doing." Carmela was back at the door. "I might have known. You promised, Perry. Sneaking around like your old man. Did you hide the bottle in the toilet tank? That's it, isn't it, Perry? Come out of there!"

Maybe some more ice-picking would help. He crawled around on the floor and felt behind the toilet until he found the ice pick, sat up with his back against the tub, and probed around in his nose. He wiped his bloody hands on his chest. More spray too. He gave his left nostril another shot of bug spray.

"Will you please please let me in, Perry," Carmela said. "I have to get dressed before Bob gets here."

"Who's Bob?" Perry's voice was weak and wet and bubbly. Why ask? Bob would be her lover, of course. He gave his right nostril a shot of bug spray. His nose felt pretty numb. Maybe if he poked the ice pick through the side of his nose, he'd surprise the buggers. Perry pushed the point of the ice pick into the side of his nose. Whoops! Bone. He moved it down to a softer spot and pushed again and felt the point break through like stabbing an orange. No pain. He wiggled the pick around and up and down, then pulled it out and did the same thing to the other side.

"Big Bob, the Bug Man. The exterminator. Don't you ever listen when I talk? I told you last night."

Last night. There was something about the head picture he'd just seen that was important to his strategy. Something about night. What was it? The dark. All the bugs playing on his face, running down his body. He wondered if Carmela ever felt them crawl across her as they left his nose to set up colonies in the apartment. They came out in the dark. That was it.

Perry scrambled around looking for the pliers. When he found them, he hugged them to his chest while he gave each of his nostrils a couple of squirts of bug spray, then he got to his feet and looked in the mirror again. There was a small jagged wound on either side of his nose and a lot of blood. He held up the pliers and snapped them open and closed a couple of times in front of his face. He remembered his plan for them. What he would do is lean in close to the mirror, poise the pliers in front of his nose, then stretch way out with his left hand and switch off the light. When he felt the bugs come out, he'd switch on the light and crush them with the pliers!

Perry put his plan into action. When he switched off the light, however, things did not get entirely dark. Blue and green fluorescent globes swam before his eyes. Some of them spun, shooting off sparks which later became globes themselves. Perry might have been lost forever, watching this light show, if he hadn't finally felt the bugs leave his nose and begin to explore his face.

Now!

He flipped on the light.

A giant roach stared back at him from the mirror.

Perry screamed, dropped the pliers, and jumped back, realizing even as he moved that what he was looking at was his own reflection. The bugs had taken over. Something in his mind must have realized that he could never beat them and had joined them. He moved his antennae experimentally and clicked and clacked his mouth parts a couple of times. My, he'd never known roaches had such big, never-blinking, brown, glassy eyes.

The doorbell rang.

"That's Bob!" Carmela said. "Now I'm going to have to meet him in my robe!"

"Don't you always?" Perry muttered. He knew he should be frightened, and he supposed he was, at least a little, but mostly the bug head seemed exactly right, the logical conclusion to this whole affair. He reached for the doorknob. Now that he had a big scary bug head, he might as well go out and have a showdown with this Bob guy. He'd take the ice pick. Maybe chase Carmela around the house a couple of times, too.

Perry eased open the door and ducked his big head as he stepped into the bedroom. He bet they'd put their heads together whispering, discussing him, no doubt, probably planning on how they could take him out of the picture. His new look would put a monkey wrench in their plans. A bigger and buggier Perry would be something new to consider. He'd expected Carmela to put his bowling bag in the middle of the room, just to taunt him, but if she had in fact peed in the bag, she'd discreetly closed the closet door on her mess. Perry moved quietly to the bedroom door and peeked out into the living room.

They weren't in the living room. Perry moved on to the kitchen. It wasn't easy to hold the weight of his new head up. He was wobbly on his feet, and everything looked a lot different through bug eyes—mostly out of focus, and he tended to see double in little fits that came and went—making navigation tricky between the coffee table and the couch, and around the glass case with Carmela's plate collection. Everything smelled of bug spray and blood. His legs were cold. Maybe he should have put on some pants.

He stepped into the kitchen. Carmela stood in her ragged pink robe fussing with the coffee pot on the stove. She'd pulled up her yellow hair and tied it on top so it looked like a geyser of straw. Perry didn't see Bob right away. In fact, it took him a few moments to puzzle out just what he was seeing. He finally decided it was a big gray butt sticking out from beneath the kitchen sink.

"Excuse me," Perry said.

Carmela jerked her head around. She yelped and dropped the coffee pot.

The butt under the sink scrambled back, and Perry saw it was a man, Big Bob, no doubt, older than Perry would have guessed, middle fifties maybe. He was dressed in gray overalls, and he dragged a silver canister and nozzle out from under the sink as he got to his feet.

"Jesus!" Bob said. "What's wrong with his nose?"

It looked to Perry like Big Bob was not so surprised as he should be, it looked, in fact, like Big Bob was fighting down a grin. Carmela, too. How could they even see his nose in his present condition?

Then it dawned on him.

Big Bob and Carmela had obviously planned the whole thing.

Picture this: Big Bob and Carmela meet at a sidewalk cafe downtown.

He's holding her hand across the table, and they drink white wine and eat thin strips of white fish with lemon wedges and sliced cucumbers. Fallen leaves rustle around their feet. The autumn sun shines in her yellow hair. A mustache flashes on and off Bob's face. Now you see it, now you don't. Tricky bastard. Bob's in the Bug Biz, and he's got contacts down South. She tells him she's so unhappy. He hands her a glass vial. Yuck, she says. From South America, he says. So how am I supposed to get them in his nose? He raises one eyebrow, says, you say he drinks? Just lets it hang there. She grins. She doesn't ask for it, but he reassures her anyway that these are strictly His and not Hers bugs. They won't get near her nose. Good news! Her grin gets wider, triumphant, and Perry sees from its very meanness something essential about her soul.

He sees the light, he learns the Lesson, and the Lesson is Life Is Like Bowling. If you're going to come out on top, you've got to keep throwing the ball.

"Maybe you better put down the ice pick," Bob said.

Time to pick up the spare. Perry ran at Big Bob.

Bob stepped to one side, swinging his nozzle up as he moved, and sprayed Perry in the face.

Perry jerked his hands up to his face and stabbed himself in the cheek with the ice pick. He stood up on his toes, windmilling his arms for balance, then fell back to his heels, and Bob gave him another squirt in the face with the bug stuff.

Real bug stuff, industrial strength. No more Mr. Grocery Store wimpy bug spray. Big Bob the Bug Man had dosed him good. Put his head in a greasy cloud. Knocked him down flat on his ass.

Perry pulled his arms in under his chin in an attitude of prayer. When the light goes on, everyone scrambles for cover, but this is what we all really want, this sweet cloud of sleep. His body shook with a sudden convulsion, and he kicked his heels against the floor. Big Bob put a big black boot on Perry's middle and pushed, and Perry did a bone crunching sit-up.

Gutter ball.

So, tell us again about the Lesson you've learned, about how Life Is Like Bowling.

Okay, okay. Forget it.

The Lesson is Life Is Nothing Like Bowling, Perry decides.

"I'll pack a bag," Carmela said.

A BREATH HOLDING CONTEST

I'll breathe through my ears and win, or I'll die. I won't give in. I
fully expect my ears to save me. It's a faith inherited from my
father who, in endless attempts to verify his theory of teleportation,
used to lurk in shadows, inside closets, behind bushes and trees,
under my bed to pop out screaming like a crack-crazed axe murderer,
hoping I'd just go somewhere else. If you're scared enough, he'd say,
your mind will move your body, Sonny. I used to think that's the way
he got rid of Mom—teleported her and her hardware-selling
boyfriend to Florida.

I've round-robined my way into the finals, and now I sit lotus
fashion on the beach in front of the local champion, a tiny whisper
of a woman like a famine victim in a yellow swim suit. She looks
familiar, but after all these years, opponents tend to blur in my mind.
Her name is Marcia, and, like me, she wears an orange scuba mask, her
mouth sealed shut with adhesive tape. She's beaming evil thoughts at
me, her beady blues narrowed but steady. She's got that "I win, you
lose" look. People tell me I wear that look, too, meaning it as an insult,

but I always take it as a compliment. Contests, any and all kinds of contests, are my meat. Marcia doesn't realize who she's dealing with.

She makes me nervous, though, and I get offensive. I put together a thought and shoot it across the space that separates us.

I can eat more jalapeno peppers than you can!

She doesn't seem impressed. This could be trouble.

I can stand on my head longer than you can, she fires back.

The spectators crouch like scavenging sea gulls on the slick, black rocks that circle Marcia and me where we sit locked in our combat, noisy as corpses with our weakly bottled up gases. The Pacific washes the rocks, but it doesn't move the onlookers, the fans, in their tennis outfits, their bikinis, their cut-off jeans and dopey hats. They shake away the salt spray and laugh. They won't admit it, but they hope one of us dies today. That's what spectators are for—to look upon the twisted, purple face of defeat and shiver deliciously.

Drops of seawater dot the glass of my mask. I smell wet rubber. I taste hospitals in the tape over my mouth. Huge hands crush my chest. I want to breathe! God, how I want it. Just to gulp in big bites of cool ocean air, smell again the pine forest lining this Oregon beach, taste the fishy sea soup in the breeze. I wouldn't turn my nose up at even the waves of sunscreen and sweat wafting from the spectators. I ache. I ache. I mustn't let it show.

I can do more one-armed pushups than you can, I tell Marcia.

I can do more tap-dance steps, she rallies.

She's got a point. If I get out of this alive, I'm going to have to bone up on my tap dancing. She knows she's scored a hit. I must work fast. I can feel the membranes that close my ears move back and forth, back and forth, holding fast. Surely they will break soon. I must be ready. When the air streams through my ears and into the back of my throat, I must play it cool, take little breaths, no great chest heaves.

I hit her with another thought. I can chug more beer than you can!

That makes her pause. I can tell a little person such as herself couldn't chug much beer.

I could run circles around your beer belly.

She's good. I decide to try another angle. I can name more vice presidents than you can!

She thinks about it. She doesn't seem worried. I have a wild moment of panic, but I fight it down. I won't give in. I'd die of shame if I lost to this woman. My vision is blurring, and muscles all over my body twitch and jerk. I make fists of my hands and put them under my thighs to hold them down. I can see that Marcia won't quit either. This is like being married again. Women just won't quit, no matter what you do to show them who can do more, who knows more, who should say what's what and when. No, they always have one more last word waiting.

I shouldn't have thought that. She jumps right on it.

I can maintain a relationship longer than you can, she tells me sweetly.

Oh, yeah!

My longest was three months.

Ah ha! Got her. My longest was six months!

I lied. My longest was a year.

I'm stunned. A year!

Marcia's turning an ugly shade of blue, and there are red blotches around her mask and tape, but I don't think I can outlast her. I must look worse. The shame sits heavy in my stomach, like too many tacos. It doesn't look like I'm going to be able to breathe through my ears after all.

You didn't last long with me, Sonny. Her thought is all ice.

That's it. She's been playing an unfair advantage. She knows me. I dig in my memory, and find her there, in Maine, that winter of the lobster-eating contest, the night we had after I beat the bib off her and everyone else.

I'm better in bed. I must make up lost ground.

I love better.

Even she must know how weak that is. She hesitates, but before I can fire another round, she gets in her best slash so far.

I know where my mother is.

That unhinges me. My brain is starving for oxygen. I shoot wild. I own the railroads. I've got Park Place!

Somehow the spectators know I've missed. They know the end is near. Her fan club chants, "Marcia! Marcia!"

Her cheeks are puffed up big, and she looks like a frog or a trumpet player, but I see the cold fire in her eyes as she delivers her coup de grâce. My father's not squatting in some doorway drinking shaving lotion and puking on his shoes!

Darts, balls, hoops, scoops, pucks! I cry. No air is ever going to come through my ears. I'm bouncing on my butt in the sand and making little whimpering sounds behind my tape. It can't end like this.

Even when you win, Sonny, you lose.

I'm snatched away like a tablecloth, leaving Marcia, the black rocks, and the spectators trembling in their places on the beach. I appear some two hundred yards up the beach on the deck of the SeaView Restaurant. I rip the mask from my face, the tape from my mouth. The air I gulp is god-I-died-and-went-to-heaven good. Thank you, Dad. Oh, thank you. Lots of eyes on me—old people in their Sunday best, young couples with wine. I see I'm about as welcome as a little accident Muffy the pooch might have left behind. A waiter is moving swiftly my way. He'll tell me to get lost, keep moving. I open my arms to the sky.

"It isn't fear that moves me, Dad," I tell him, wherever he is. "It's chagrin."

FANCY PANTS

He pulled into the repair lane and stopped. She twisted around in the passenger seat to look back, ready to give him the signal, and he stared down the exit ramp watching the bridge. They didn't worry about the complicated cloverleaf above them. The trick was to wait for a gap in traffic and then make a dash for it. At this time of morning, it wouldn't take long.

"Now," she said.

"No good," he said, meaning either there were too many cars coming the other way on the freeway or too much activity down on the bridge. Someone might see them enter the secret place. There would never be a time with no traffic at all, but it was only the close traffic they worried about. Anyone seeing them leave the road from a distance might not believe their eyes or more likely would pretend they hadn't seen it at all.

A few moments later she said, "Go."

This time it was okay. He stepped on the gas and speeded onto the exit ramp, but instead of continuing to the bridge below, he suddenly pulled off the road and down the steep embankment. This was the tricky part. If he didn't hit the exact spot, they would probably crack up, damage the car, maybe hurt themselves. Certainly they'd have to call someone and make explanations.

But he'd gotten it right again. They bounced over the uneven ground, down the green slope of wild grasses and dandelions, down into a space that was surrounded on all sides by highways but was lower than them all, a hidden valley in the city. At the bottom, the freeway itself was some fifty yards above, the exit ramp twenty yards up, and the cross street running along the bridge maybe thirty yards above them. There was a tight line of trees on the freeway side.

In the valley itself, more trees and shrubs grew. He tucked the car into a place he knew could not be seen even if someone stopped and walked around the perimeter of the secret place as he had done once after parking and climbing back up the embankment.

He got out of the car. The air was cool, and he could smell a farm somewhere, or at least cows, or at least things that crapped wherever they were standing, whenever they felt like it. Or maybe he was smelling a memory. He leaned back down to give her a smile where she still sat looking straight ahead in the shotgun seat.

"I need to use the bathroom," she said.

"So, use the bushes," he said. " You could have gone before we left the house." He walked around the car and opened the trunk.

She got out and slammed her door, and the sound was loud enough to silence the birds and bugs for a moment. She came to him and looked down into the trunk and hugged herself as the wind blew her skirt around her legs.

"Where did the chairs come from?" she asked.

"Wherever chairs come from." He grabbed one of the wooden chairs and pulled it from the trunk. He set it on its feet and then reached in for the other one.

116

There was a big brown wicker picnic basket.

"Here I'll take that," she said.

"I thought you had to use the bathroom?"

"I can wait a few minutes." She took the basket from him and moved into the trees. He picked up the chairs and followed her.

They walked through waist-high grass and then thorny under-growth for a small distance and came to a meadow. The bridge was directly overhead. There was a brook with tiny silver and blue fish darting about. He put the chairs down beside the water.

"No, over here," she said.

She shook out a big red, green, and white checked blanket and let it settle to the grass like a magic carpet. He carried the chairs over and put them on the blanket. She slipped off into the forest, and a moment later he could see a bush quivering like there were many frightened quail in there, instead of just her, peeing.

He sat down on one of the chairs. A moment later, she returned and knelt on the blanket. She opened the picnic basket and took out a black case longer than his forearm. You had to wonder how it fit in there. She handed it to him. He put it on his lap and opened it. Inside were the three silver pieces of a flute. The sight of the gleaming instrument sent a little shiver of anticipation down his spine, and he looked up at her and smiled.

She had taken her place on the other chair, the bow of her cello poised to play over the instrument itself.

"Where did the cello come from?" he asked.

"Wherever cellos come from," she said.

"What about the wine and cheese and baguettes?"

"Later," she said.

He lifted the flute to his mouth and ran through several scales to loosen up. "Okay?" he said.

She answered by drawing the bow across the strings of her cello.

He listened for a moment, then stepped in just where he was expected. Vivaldi. Late in a concerto in G minor. Allegro.

"You flute guys are the best when it comes to oral sex," she said.

He blew a low, middle, and high F justlikethat, and she laughed, but you had to wonder how he was hearing her over the music.

"My Russian grandmother used to say look for a fellow who plays the flute."

You had to wonder if her Russian grandmother had had oral sex in mind when she used to say that.

She said, "It has everything to do with lip control. All your little flourishes."

Yes, her lips were moving so he probably wasn't reading her mind. He might have made a snappy comeback, but his mouth was busy with the flute.

"It's that fine control of air," she said. "Like a thin thread tickling from the lips, moving here and there, just there. They say you guys develop muscles you don't use for anything else but flute playing. Little do they know. And I haven't said a word about tonguing."

She laughed again, a high soprano laugh that blended perfectly with the music, and he felt absolutely wonderful. Bluebirds hopped out onto their branches to whistle along with the music. Squirrels came out to swing and sway. Grinning raccoons gathered at the edge of the blanket.

"Aren't we happy?" she asked, and then she answered herself, "Yes, we're so very very happy."

Danger. Danger.

Hadn't he warned her that if you do so much smiling your face might freeze like that, and then where would you be? She wouldn't listen.

"So very happy."

She sounded a little desperate.

He could see that her hands were already bleeding. With every stroke of the bow across the strings, she left a smear of aggressive red blood across the smooth wooden face of the cello.

He was in no better shape. He could see now in blurry close-up the contrast of his own blood on the silver flute keys. That contrast reminded him of the difference between the meat and the machine, the knife and the muscle, a sudden silver slice across the vein.

Her nose fell off.

She looked startled for a moment, but she didn't stop playing. He could feel his face slipping. He smiled. A mistake. He knew all that smiling would get him in trouble. He saw her eyes widen a little, and he figured he must look pretty frightful.

"Lend me your ears," he said, and she grinned sadly, then hugely as the meat of her cheeks popped off like hubcaps from explosive high speed blowouts—both sides at once, and she might have lost control, might have missed a beat, botched a note, but she didn't, and he was proud of her control and hoped his would be as good. It was getting hard to hold the slippery bleeding fish his flute had become.

Her hair slipped forward into her eyes, and she shook it away, and it flew from her like a startled brown cat. They bled and bled until there was nothing left to bleed. Their picnic looked like the site of a barnyard butchering or the scene of a ghastly murder. The two wooden chairs on the bloody blanket.

All of that meat.

The flute (now part of his metal arm) became a steel hammer.

She stood up, and her cello became her hips, the rich wood dulled to tin and rusting.

"I don't understand why I'm not totally freaked by this," she said.

"It all seems somehow familiar," he said.

"You look like a bunch of spare parts," she said.

"I think we should find something to wear." His voice crackled and popped.

"Fig leaves," she said. A seam opened around the equator of her head, and the northern hemisphere swung up and away over the dark cave of her new mouth.

"Would you knock off all the goofy smiling?" he said.

He dug into a pile of tin boxes, broken mirrors, and oily rags and came up with a pair of fuzzy pants.

"Hey, these look good," he said.

"Too fancy," she said and nudged him aside to dig in the pile. "This will do." She held up a pair of ragged gray slacks. "Oh, and look, a box of shoes. Watch out. I'm going to smile again!"

"Very funny," he said.

He got into his fuzzy pants; she got into her gray slacks. They picked out shoes. They walked back to the bloody blanket.

He leaned over and picked up a few scraps of flesh. "Don't you want to keep your face?"

She made a dismissive gesture with the hook at the end of her left arm.

"Well, I do," he said. He put his face back on his metal head, but it wouldn't stay there. After picking it up off the ground a couple of times, he tucked the hair above his old forehead into the waistband of his new pants, and his face hung down like a short apron.

The raccoons were just spare parts now, but the squirrels had mostly held their shapes. He picked up a mechanical squirrel head and put it on his pants. It stayed where he put it, as if his pants had been waiting for the carcass all along. He added another squirrel head along with what might have been an old clock or the happy face of a beaver. He plucked a windup bluebird hanging upside down from the grove of TV antennas and stuck it to his pants. He hooked a monkey playing cymbals over the pocket in back where he once would have carried a wallet.

The brook was now a sluggish stream running from the side of a hill of oil drums. On all sides, the debris was heaped so high you could only see a patch of smoky sky. Piles of old French horns, bent trombones and tubas hid the car. He pulled the horns down and crushed them underfoot and made a path. She followed.

The car looked like a thing that had never moved. It might have been a big soda can crushed by a giant. A fan of broken glass spread out in front of it.

He got in behind the wheel. She wrenched the passenger door off and got it, too.

"What now?" she asked.

"I don't know," he said.

He put the hammer at the end of his arm on top of the steering wheel.

"Do you want to hear my theory?" he asked.

She sighed.

"I'll take that as a yes," he said. "My theory is that when it became possible to exchange our biological bodies for mechanical bodies that might last forever, because you could always get spare parts for them, we were the first on our block to do it."

"I suppose that does sound like us," she said.

"Of course, there was the matter of expense," he said.

"Yes," she said. "Life is always about money."

He knocked himself on the head with his hammer, and it sounded like a dull gong. "I mean, how much do you suppose we could afford to spend on these?"

"Not much, if you ask me," she said.

"Not to mention the integrity of the flesh that seemed to be layered over the basic frame."

"Yes, let's not mention that," she said.

"So, my theory is that our illusions have been repossessed," he said.

"How do you mean?"

"We're like this," he said, "because the bank or whoever has come and taken back all of our pretty fantasies."

"There's a name for the trouble with your theory," she said.

"Oh? And would you like to enlighten me on just what that could be?"

"It's called the Continuity Problem," she said. "If, as you say, we were once biological and we decided to move, so to speak, how do we know we're the same people?"

"I don't see the problem," he said.

"Let's suppose our brain patterns were duplicated exactly and ported into our new hardware," she said.

"Right. That's just what I'm saying."

"Okay," she said. "So, at some point our patterns must have existed both in our old heads and in some device at the same time."

"So?"

"So, was it really you in your old head or was it you in the new device?"

"Both," he said.

"But, the old biological you didn't continue into the new mechanical you," she said. "From those people's viewpoints we simply died. That's the problem with your theory. We wouldn't really be ourselves."

"That could be true, you know," he said. "We might not be our old selves."

"But it isn't true," she said. "I think we've always been as we are. My theory is that someone is beaming evil illusions at us this very moment!"

"You're thinking we're not really robots?"

"And we never have been robots," she said. "We think we're like this because some malevolent force is imposing dreams on us. It's a trick."

"Nonsense," he said. "Your theory demands some evil outside force beaming illusions at us. Metaphysical hocus pocus."

"Your theory," she said, "demands some evil outside force repossessing our illusions—some silly cyber-repo-man."

They spent a few quiet moments staring out the empty front window at the freeway pileup the world had become.

"Our beautiful life," she said. "The house. Your wonderful job."

"I managed a hamburger joint," he said.

"Yes, but it was a very good hamburger joint."

"It's nice of you to say so," he said.

"The music," she said.

"I suppose we should try to climb out of here," he said.

"We could just sit here until it goes away," she said.

"I really don't think it's going to go away," he said.

"You'll see," she said.

"Fat chance," he said.

"Those horrible pants," she said.

"Look who's talking," he said.

Her head burst into flames.

"Watch it!" He scrambled out of the car. A moment later she got out, too. Flames raged up from her head.

That was so just like her, he thought and turned and walked toward the embankment.

"Hey!" she said. "Hey! You can't set my head on fire and just walk off. Come back here!"

"What do you want from me?" he said without turning to look back at her. He didn't stop walking. "This is the best we could do." Why was she blaming him for her head anyway? Her fire and his hot words could be totally coincidental.

"Please." There was something in her tone, something helpless, something speaking to their long history which had not always been happy, but had been often good, or at least not too bad most of the time.

He signed. He turned. He would have recognized her anywhere. Even without flesh. Maybe it was the way she stood, her shoulders slumped, her metal head ablaze.

"Bang it," he said, "maybe you can put it out if you bang it."

"I won't bang it," she said.

"Oh, all right," he said. "Okay. Hold still." He walked back to her.

He had no lungs and couldn't blow, and when he waved his hands and slapped at the flames, they just got bigger, so maybe it was good he couldn't blow. He glanced around the junkyard and spotted a bent and rusted metal bucket. "Hold on," he said.

He dumped nails and dirt from the bucket and put it over her head.

"How's that?" he asked.

"I don't think it's working." Her voice was muffled.

She was probably right. There were still a few flames licking out of the black smoke billowing from under the rim of the bucket.

"Grab on," he said. "Maybe it'll go out as we walk."

She groped around blindly and then seized him with the alligator clip of her right hand.

He led her around the perimeter of their secret place. Piled high on all sides were mountains of oil drums and old tires, hills of twisted metal lawn furniture. Smashed television sets. Piles of kitchen gadgets. Steam whistles. Buckets of bolts and pails of nails. Dead cars and broken bicycles.

There were no sounds from the freeway above, no sounds from the exit ramp, no sounds from the bridge. If there were other machines out there, they weren't making any noise.

"My peacock," she said.

"Will you get off the subject of my pants?" he asked.

"Who said anything about your pants?"

"Maybe your head would go out if you didn't talk so much," he said.

They made another circuit around the junkyard. There was no easy way out, no gentle slope, no simple climb. He took her back to the blanket. Most of the meat was gone, some stains, bits that might be meat and might be metal. "Sit down," he said and guided her into a chair. "I want to see how hard it would be to climb the slope."

He walked back to exit ramp-side. The distance here should be the shortest. He took a look back at her sitting with her hands folded in her lap, a little black smoke still drifting from under the bucket over her head. A mechanical woman in a metal garden waiting for her mechanical man to come back so they could open their wicker-wire picnic basket and eat aluminum foil sandwiches. Someone should do a painting.

He looked up the slope. He couldn't tell where the top was. It might go on forever. He bent at the waist and put the hammer at the end of his arm down on an oil drum. It rolled away from him, and he fell. He got up and tried again, and brought an avalanche of junk down on top of himself. He fought his way to the surface. His body was just not built for scrambling up hills of junk.

He could probably keep bringing down the junk on his head until he made a path through to the dirt, but it would take a long time. And then what? He had a sudden picture of himself crawling to the top at last and looking down at her and realizing that she couldn't climb out and he couldn't climb back down.

He wouldn't let that be the way they ended.

He went back to her. She was humming something under her bucket. There wasn't much smoke now.

He walked around the edge of the blanket, righting the upside-down windup birds on the TV antennas. He lined up the mechanical squirrel skulls and cobbled together enough old parts to make a couple of raccoons, if you knew they were supposed to be raccoons and didn't look too closely and weren't too critical.

He sat down on the other chair.

He leaned forward and pulled the bucket from her head. "Raccoons," he said.

Her head split open in a smile.

He turned the bucket upside down and held it between his knees and tapped out a rhythm with his hammer.

"Our music," he said.

"La la. La la," she sang.

IN THE REFRIGERATOR

So I come home to find her sitting on the hide-a-bed with this brown paper bag over her head. She hasn't turned on the lights. There are shadows everywhere. I can just make out the name of the grocery store printed in upside-down letters on the front of the bag. She's wearing one of the big bags.

"What are you doing?" I say.

"Don't talk to me," she says.

I reach across her and turn on the table lamp. I see that she's wearing basketball shoes untied, and that her hands are folded in her lap.

I look her up and down, becoming strangely aroused, knowing that she knows I'm looking at her but can't look back.

"I'm looking at you," I say.

"Leave me alone."

I sit down beside her, being careful not to touch her but sitting close enough on the sagging couch to make her lean in my direction. She moves away from me in prissy little annoyed scoots. Her bag wobbles, but when she's gotten as far from me as she can, she straightens it, then puts her hands back in her lap. I sigh and settle back with my arm across the top of the couch, my hand just behind her head. I stretch out my legs. They don't quite reach the opposite wall. Otherwise, we'd never be able to fold the couch out into a bed at night. I could reach to my side and take something from our tiny refrigerator if there was anything I wanted in our tiny refrigerator. The place smells of her. The place smells of me. It's uniquely our smell now, merged in the end by these close walls.

I sigh again, knowing she'll know I'm sighing at her.

I get no response. It's as if she is in another room instead of sitting right beside me on the couch with a paper bag over her head.

"So have you been sitting here with that bag over your head all afternoon?" I say.

She says, "I heard you coming up the stairs."

I say, "You heard me coming and you hurried over to the couch and put a grocery bag over your head?"

"Yes," she says.

I suppose what she's doing makes some sense. In fact, nothing she does makes absolutely no sense. We live in a single room. We cook here, we sleep here, we do everything here. Well, we do go down the hall to use the bathroom we share with another couple. But there aren't many chances to be alone.

"Let me see your face," I say.

"Go away," she says.

"I think we should hash this out," I say.

She doesn't answer, and her silence infuriates me. I lean in close to snatch the bag from her head, but stop myself just in time.

"Come out of there!" I say.

"I won't," she says.

I take a deep breath. I count to ten. I do some deep knee bends. I root around under the sink and find a paper bag of my own. I wait to unfold it until I'm standing right in front of her again. I want her to hear the sound.

It doesn't make enough noise when I unfold it. So I shake it. I can see it is having an effect on her by the way she squeezes her hands into fists in her lap.

I sit back down beside her.

"Okay," I say, "you want to be alone, I'll just go off by myself." I shake the bag again and then put it over my head. I am startled by all the room inside. "Hey, there's really a lot of room in here!" I say, and as I speak I can hear my voice is different, and I realize that she can probably hear that my voice sounds different now, too. I picture her sitting there beside me with the bag over her head, wondering just what I'm up to. Has she figured it out yet? Is she sitting there picturing me sitting here with a bag over my own head? Or has she taken her bag off?

I worry that maybe she is looking at me now.

As if to confirm my fears, I hear her get to her feet and open the refrigerator.

Then I hear nothing at all.

I don't even hear the refrigerator close.

I listen carefully. But I cannot tell what is going on. Is there any-one out there? I'm afraid to look. I'm afraid to know.

THE PERECT GIFT

The children had stuffed their ragged clothes with newspaper against the snow that Christmas eve. Tim still had on his dirty Dodgers cap, and you could see Amy's mousy hair through the holes in her summer scarf. They huddled together on the curb in the moonlight, waiting for Santa, blowing into their hands, rubbing one another's shoulders, listening to their chattering teeth, listening to their rumbling bellies.

"Me, I want cake," Amy said.

"I want a burger," Tim said. "I want some fries and a Coke and maybe one of those one-man pies."

"Cake," Amy said. "Chocolate cake."

Soon headlights appeared moving slowly down the dark street. The children could hear the tires in the oily slush of melted snow.

"Get ready to run," Tim said. "In case it's not him." He took her hand and they got their feet.

The big white limo with the two red you-better-watch-out eyes on the door pulled up beside them, and Santa climbed out of the back seat.

"Merry Christmas!" His voice boomed and echoed in the carcasses of the burnt-out buildings lining the street. He dragged his big sack out on the sidewalk. "I'll bet you two have been good this year," he said. "Is that true?"

"Yes!" the children cried.

Santa gave them a stern look, but they knew he didn't mean it. "Maybe I should check my book."

"No!"

"You're right. No need to look. I remember you two." The jolly old gentleman dug into his big red sack of Christmas goodies. "Let me see. Let me see." He finally found what he wanted and straightened up again. "Here you go, young man." He handed Tim a big card, maybe four or five inches high and eight or so long. "And one for you, Missy."

Tim looked down at his card. It was smooth and slippery. Glossy. There was a picture of several cooked birds surrounded by greenery on a white plate. There was a border of little blue flowers all around the card. Along the top were the words GREAT RECIPES OF THE WORLD. There were instructions. The ingredients were in bold letters. A snowflake fell onto the card and melted, but the card was so slick, the snowflake couldn't wet it. What Tim liked best about the card was that it was new; it had no sad history. Tim looked at Amy, then they both looked back up at Santa.

"I can see you're wondering," Santa said. "It's like this." He put his hand on Tim's shoulder. "If you give a man food, he can eat for a day, but if you teach him to cook, well, dot dot dot!"

"Dot dot dot?" Tim asked.

"Yes," Santa said with a bit of an edge to his voice. "Dot dot dot!"

Tim and Amy knew just how to talk to grownups. "Thank you, Santa," they said together.

Santa treated them to a few ho ho hos, and his bowl full of jelly routine, then climbed back into his car. The limo sloshed on down the street.

When the car disappeared, Tim and Amy settled back down onto the cold curb.

"What'd you get?" Tim asked.

"Casserole of Octopus," Amy said. "Looks squishy. What about you?"

"Braised Squabs."

"What's a squab?"

"I don't know. Looks like little chickens in the picture."

"Timmy?"

"Yeah?"

"Wanna trade?"

Tim pretended to think about it for a moment, and it wasn't all pretend, then he put his arm around her shoulders and pulled her in close. "Anything for you, kiddo," he said.

MESSAGE IN A FISH

The phone rang three more times before Josh decided it wasn't part of the elaborate dream he was dreaming of Valerie and got up to answer it. As he stumbled into the living room, he thought the phone would almost certainly stop ringing just as he picked it up, so there was no need to hurry. He had time to run through a short list of people who might be calling him at a time like this: someone else had died, probably Aunt Eppie, or maybe it was a collections guy—Josh hadn't made payments on anything in months, or a wrong number, or a crank call—some serious heavy breathing or Prince Albert in a can (or maybe it would be Valerie calling from the Starship. See? I'm not so dead after all!). He picked up the phone, and said hello.

"So, you the guy with the fish?"

"What?" Josh stood on one foot so he could pick the other one up off the cold wooden floor. In the dark, the hum and splash of his fish tanks sounded like a creek cascading over smooth rocks. It might be a chilly night in the rain forest along the Rio Negro—were there ever any chilly nights in South America? And what was this about a fish?

Oh yeah, the fish. His classified would have appeared in today's paper. Good god, why was he still in bed? He pushed the little button on the side of his watch and saw that it was four-thirty in the morning. "Do you know what time it is?"

"Have you mistaken me for the Time Lady?" The caller sounded like a man Josh wouldn't want to get to know. "Did you advertise the fish or not?"

"I did," Josh said. "I just didn't expect people to be calling up in the middle of the night. And who's the Time Lady?"

"Just how many people do you think will be calling at all for an item like this?"

"Lots!" Josh said. Who wouldn't be fascinated by Cosmo? He was a beautiful and very rare fish. To see him was to love him. If things had not been so very desperate, Josh would not have placed the classified at all, but now that he had, he was sure people would be lining up around the block just to get a look. Josh would have to sell tickets, maybe hold an auction. It was not like such fish were falling out of the sky.

"In your dreams," the caller said.

"Are you sure you know what we're talking about here? If you're just looking for something to swim around and look pretty, maybe you should try your local pet shop."

"What I want to know is does it have lips yet?" the caller asked.

Okay, clearly the man knew which way the wind was blowing. Only people familiar with the Top Hat Fish would ask about the lips, and not only the lips themselves, but the timing of their appearance. An amateur would have asked about the hat.

"He's just getting lips," Josh said.

There were so many things to know about Cosmo. Probably the

most common blunder was to confuse him with a common arowana (Osteoglossum bicirrhosum). Not that the arowana wasn't an interesting fish in its own right. Often described as "prehistoric," arowanas were imported into the pet shop trade from South America. They grew to a length of about 20 inches in captivity and preferred large live foods like goldfish, but they could also be trained to take chunks of raw fish or beef. They were sleek and graceful and were often displayed in big tanks in Chinese restaurants. In the wild they leaped out of the water to snatch bugs and small birds from overhanging branches. In captivity they often leaped out of their tanks and flopped around on the floor and died.

Your garden variety arowana was no Top Hat Fish (Osteoglossum sombreroium) like Cosmo. Cosmo was two feet long and pearly white with rose highlights and blue eyes. And the hat, of course. The reason the Top Hat Fish was called the Top Hat Fish was the black growth on the top of its head. The growth developed slowly (like the lips) but in adult specimens looked just like a black satin evening hat.

"So you're saying the fish has no lips," the caller said. "Okay, so how about the hat? Are you sure you've got a true Top Hat? It's an easy mistake to make when you're new at this."

"I'm not new at this," Josh said. "The hat is around two inches high and maybe an inch in diameter. It is jet black and perfectly formed."

"In that case I'll give you a hundred dollars for the fish."

"You've got to be kidding," Josh said.

"Look, you know and I know no one else is going to call on this."

"You're not even in the ball park," Josh said. "This isn't bargaining. I don't even hear you yet."

"I think my offer is pretty reasonable," the caller said, "considering the fact that you've probably taken an ordinary arowana and superglued Ken's black plastic ballroom-dancing hat to its head."

"What!"

"I've always wondered how you guys get the fish to hold still while the glue dries."

"What are you talking about?" Josh wished he were dressed. If he weren't standing in the dark in his underwear he might be able to handle this.

"And how do you get the fish's head dry enough for the glue to take in the first place? A blow dryer?"

"Are you crazy?"

"Okay," the caller said, "make it a hundred and fifty."

Josh banged the phone down. Banging it down felt so good that he picked it up and banged it down again. It didn't feel quite as good the second time. He was trembling. The very idea!

He walked back to his bedroom and got his robe. It had been a crank call after all. He sat down on the edge of the bed. He wouldn't be able to go back to sleep. Valerie would have told him not to brood, and she would have kept after him until he smiled. His reaction to the unusual had always cracked her up. But she had followed an idiot into oblivion (or joined the Others on the Starship, depending on how you looked at it) and he would have to deal with this alone. He went back into the living room and switched on the lights in all of the fish tanks.

Cosmo came out to take a look.

The fish was a vision of grace, Josh thought, a rosy pearl water snake with fins. At unpredictable times Cosmo rolled in the water like a kayak. That roll might lead someone who didn't know any better to think that the black hat on his head was in fact artificial, that it had been added by some crazy person, that it was knocking the fish's sense of balance out of kilter. Such things were not unheard of. Just look at the way people colored fish and called them "painted perch."

Josh had a moment of doubt. What if Cosmo were not a sombreroium after all? In fact, what if every Top Hat Fish he'd ever seen had been a fake? All that talk about a new species that seemed not to be altogether of this Earth might just be a lot of hot air. What if Cosmo were a bicirrhosum that someone had altered? How could that have happened? Well, for starters, the collector he'd bought the fish from would have had to be in on it. Wilkins was a man Josh had long trusted as a reliable source, but even a reliable source could be corrupted. Suppose someone comes to Wilkins and says hey we'll give you this suitcase stuffed with money or maybe we won't kill your kidnapped family if you convince Josh Torbert this common arowana is a rare and wonderful Top Hat Fish. Next someone would have had to break into his house and glue the plastic top hat to the fish's head at just the time when a real sombreroium would have developed the characteristic satiny black growth. Was that why he couldn't get in touch with Wilkins? Could it be that Wilkins was not really off on a collecting trip in Southeast Asia as his wife claimed? Or might this whole thing have something to do with Valerie and her circle of dead space cadets?

Was Cosmo really developing lips? Ordinary arowanas had no lips—in fact they had large top-opening mouths that they used to scoop things off the surface of the water. Unlike the sombreroium whose face would flatten and who would slowly come to resemble a jowly man (say Richard Nixon), the arowana would never develop lips. So what about Cosmo? Josh got down on his knees to look at Cosmo's lips.

The phone rang.

"Okay, maybe that crack about the glue was out of line." It was the same man. "Are you there?"

"I'm here," Josh said.

"So look, I'm sorry about that. Hey, I don't even know your name. Tell me your name."

"Josh Torbert."

"And the address."

Josh gave him his address and then regretted it at once.

"Okay, Josh, enough joking around. Here's my real offer for the fish, assuming it is in fact in good shape and developing lips. Are you ready for my offer?"

"I'm ready," Josh said. This could be it. Maybe the ad had worked after all. Maybe the conversation before had been some kind of test. Maybe the caller would now name a figure that would bail Josh out of all his debts. The back payments on the TV. (Why hadn't the man named the figure yet?) It might be big enough to cover the missing mortgage payments. The bank had already filed the papers on the house, but that didn't mean it was too late. Maybe he could even cover Valerie's final expenses. (Why hadn't the man named the figure yet? Had the two of them entered into some kind of weird time warp? Would Josh remain forever listing the things that he could pay off with the money?) Maybe there would be enough left over to pack up the rest of the fish and get out of town. Make a clean getaway—maybe get a van and revisit all of their favorites spots from Shasta to the red cliffs of Sedona. He looked over at Cosmo and saw that the fish was floating upside down, belly to the sky, hat pointed at the bottom. The kayak business again, this time not flipping over so fast, nothing to panic about, normal for the breed. (Why hadn't the man named the figure?) Cosmo rolled upright, and Josh saw that the fish's lips had become more developed just in the time he had been on pins and needles waiting for the man to name the figure that would chase his financial blues away.

"Two hundred dollars."

"What?" Josh shouted. He took the phone away from his ear and looked at it then put it back to his ear. "What?"

"Two hundred," the man said. "It's a fair price considering that I am the only game in town."

"Ten times that would still be an insult."

"Two hundred and fifty dollars," the man said.

Josh hung up.

Still on his knees, he moved closer to Cosmo's tank and put his face very near the glass. Cosmo, in his top hat and tails, like maybe he'd be stepping out tonight, swam up to the glass. Josh looked closely at his new lips and saw that the fish was now forming a single word over and over again.

What was Cosmo trying to say?

The phone rang.

Josh leaned away from the tank and picked it up.

"Look, I know who you are," the man said. "I know where you live."

Josh dropped the phone and scooted quickly back to the fish tank. Cosmo seemed to be saying something more complicated now. Josh concentrated as hard as he could, but he could not read the fish's lips. He was distracted by a small voice shouting from somewhere far away. He picked up the phone again.

"Josh, Josh?"

"I'm here," Josh said.

"Forget what I said about the fire."

"The fire?"

"I said forget about the fire," the man said. "Let me tell you something you may not know about your fish."

"I doubt you know anything about my fish that I don't know," Josh said.

"Certain reliable sources believe the Osteoglossum sombreroium is not rightly named," the man said. "There are those who think the family is wrong, that it should be perhaps Synodontis or more likely Corydoras sombreroium."

"Nonsense," Josh said. "You're trying to tell me the Top Hat Fish is a cat fish?"

"Exactly," the man said. "So you see my offers have not been so far off the mark. Let me try another figure on you."

"You're an idiot," Josh said.

"Three hundred dollars."

Josh hung up.

He would unplug the phone. He grabbed the cord to follow it down to the wall, but before he got there, he stepped on something sharp, yelped and dropped the cord. He sat down on the floor to look at his foot. Just below the big toe of his right foot was a crescent cut, a bloody half moon. He pressed the edge of his robe against it to stop the bleeding and felt around on the floor for whatever he'd stepped on.

Once he found it, he didn't know what he was looking at. He turned the object over and over in front of his face; he moved it away for a more distant view, and then brought it in close. When it dawned on him what he was holding, he gasped.

A tiny yellow plastic fez.

From where he sat he saw something else gleaming on the carpet. He got to his knees and crawled over to it.

A little gray plastic fedora.

And over there. He could see a line of colorful spots leading away from Cosmo's tank. He crawled down the line of little hats.

A tiny white straw boater.

A flat black pill box.

A beanie no bigger than the pad of his thumb.

A green cloche.

A petite red beret.

The very essence of Cosmo was spreading across his living room floor toward the other fish tanks. Perhaps this was only the beginning of The Great Event Valerie and her friends had been always going on about. Maybe, someday soon, all the fish of the world would wear hats, and the Starship would swing back around the sun to pick up the people left behind last time.

The phone rang.

Josh crawled back to Cosmo's tank. He sat down and leaned back against the tank stand and picked up the phone.

"Okay, Josh," the caller said, "we've had our fun, haven't we? I'll come over and if your fish measures up, I'll write you a check on the spot for one thousand dollars. What do you say?"

It probably was a reasonable offer. He wouldn't be able to pay off many bills but maybe he could get a head start when he left town. Something in the man's voice told him that this was the last offer.

From behind him came the sound of a fingernail tapping on the glass of a fish tank. He shuddered. Valerie used to do that. It drove the fish crazy. He twisted around to look.

Cosmo tapped the glass again with his top hat. Josh put the phone down and leaned forward until he and the fish were face to face with only a small space and the glass between them. Cosmo was desperately trying to tell him something, his new lips forming the same phrase over and over again. Something something something something something VALERIE.

There was no doubt. Cosmo was talking about Valerie.

The fish repeated the message, and Josh got the first word and said, "CAN'T something something something something VALERIE."

Cosmo swam in a circle and then returned to repeat the message.

CAN'T YOU something something something VALERIE.

Yes, he almost had it.

CAN'T YOU something IT'S something VALERIE.

Then he got it.

CAN'T YOU SEE IT'S ME VALERIE!

Cosmo was channeling Valerie! He might have known she'd do

something weird like this. In fact he would have been disappointed by an ordinary haunting.

There was more.

Now that he had gotten the hang of Cosmo's lips, reading the next utterance was a piece of cake: DON'T SELL THE FISH!

Either Valerie had come home and was speaking through Cosmo, or Cosmo had come up with this scheme to save himself all on his own. In either case, Josh couldn't sell him now.

He picked up the phone and said, "Hello."

"Josh! I thought you hung up on me again."

"Look, the fish is no longer for sale."

"I'm sorry to hear you say that," the man said.

"I'm sorry, too," Josh said.

"I warn you," the man said. "There will be repercussions."

"I know," Josh said. He hung up and then stepped carefully around all the little hats and unplugged the phone.

He settled back down in front of Cosmo's tank. "So, how are things on the Starship?" he asked.

CATCH

Your face, I say, is a wild animal this morning, Lucy, and I'm glad it's caged. Her scowl is so deep I can't imagine she's ever been without it. Her yellow hair is a frumpy halo around her wire mask. My remark doesn't amuse her.

I know what I did. I just don't know why it pissed her off, and if I don't know, insensitive bastard that I am, she certainly isn't going to tell me.

She lifts the cat over her head and hurls it at me. Hurls it hard. I catch it and underhand it back to her. The cat is gray on top and snowy white below and mostly limp, its eyes rolled back in its head and its coated tongue hanging loose out of one side of its mouth. I know from experience that it will die soon, and its alarm collar will go off, and one of us will toss it into the ditch that runs between us. A fresh angry bundle of teeth and claws will drop from the hatch in the ceiling, and we'll toss the new cat back and forth between us until our staggered breaks, when other catchers take our places. The idea is to keep the animals in motion twenty-four hours a day.

In this profession, we wear canvas shirts and gloves and wire cages over our faces. I sometimes dream we've lost our jobs, Lucy and me. What a nightmare. What else do we know? My replacement comes in behind me. He takes up the straw broom and dips it into the water in the ditch that runs through the toss-box and sweeps at the smeared feces and urine staining the floor and walls. A moment later, the buzzer sounds, and he puts the broom back in the corner. I step aside, and Lucy tosses the cat to him. I slip out of the box and into the catacomb for my fifteen minute break before moving on to the next box.

Lucy and I work an hour on and fifteen minutes off all day long. As we move from toss-box to toss-box, our paths cross and recross. I'll be out of phase with her for half an hour, probably just long enough for her to work up a real rage.

The catacomb is a labyrinth of wide tunnels dotted with concrete boxes. There is a metal chute running from the roof to the top of each box. The boxes are evenly spaced, and there is a light bulb for every box, but not all the bulbs are alive so there are gaps in the harsh light. The boxes are small rooms, and there is a wooden door on each side so catchers can be replaced without interrupting the tossing. The concrete walls of the tunnels, like the concrete walls of the boxes, are streaked black and white and beaded with moisture. The floors are roughened concrete. Everything smells like wet rocks and dead things.

So what did I do?

While Lucy dressed for work this morning, I played with our infant daughter, Megan, tossing her into the air and catching her again, blowing bubbles into her stomach while she pulled my hair and giggled until she got the hiccups.

When Lucy came in, I tossed the baby in a high arc across the room to her. Megan tumbled in a perfect backward somersault in the air. Lucy went dead white. She snatched Megan out of the air and hugged the child to her chest.

"Nice catch," I said.

"Don't you ever," Lucy said, her voice all husky and dangerous, "ever do that again, Desmond! Not ever."

Then she stomped out taking Megan with her.

What the hell? I'd known there was no chance whatever that Lucy would miss. She's a professional. My trusting her to catch the love of my life, the apple of my eye, Daddy's little girl, was, I thought, a pretty big compliment. Lucy didn't buy it. In fact, she didn't even let me explain at all, said instead, oh shut up, Desmond, just shut up, and off we went to work, silent, stewing, our hurt feelings like a sack of broken toys between us.

Now she's not speaking to me. It's going to be a long day.

The buzzer sounds, and I move into the next box. I do my duty with the broom, and when the buzzer sounds again I replace the catcher. The cat here is a howling orange monster, and I have my hands full. When the animal is this fresh, the tossing technique looks a lot like volleyball. You don't want to be too close to the thing for very long.

By the time Lucy takes her place across from me, I've established a rhythm and am even able to put a little spin on the cat now and then. I have to hand it to Lucy. She catches up quickly, and soon we have the animal sailing smoothly between us.

The animals go through stages as we toss and catch them. First defiance, then resistance, followed by resignation, then despair, and finally death. This one is probably somewhere in the resistance stage, not fighting wildly, but watching for an opening to do some damage. I put one hand on the cat's chest and the other under its bottom and send it across to Lucy in a sitting position. Not to be outdone she sends it back still sitting but upside down now. Maybe the silly positions have done the trick. Whatever. I can feel the animal slip into the resignation stage.

I toss the cat tumbling head over heels, a weak howl and a loose string of saliva trailing behind it. Is Lucy ever going to talk to me again?

"Okay, I'm sorry," I say, giving in to the idea that I might never know exactly why I should be sorry.

I see tears come to her eyes, and she falters, nearly drops the cat. I want to go to her. I want to comfort her, but it will be some time before we're both on a break at the same time, and I see suddenly that it will be too late by then. It simply won't matter anymore.

My replacement comes in and sweeps up. Then the buzzer sounds. I step aside.

Lucy isn't crying anymore.

I reach for the door.

THE FINGER

Bobby wanted to practice it on his mother, but he knew her face would turn red, then purple, and he'd see all the veins pulsing in her head. Smoke would pour from her ears and nose. Her eyes would pinwheel, and sparks would fly. Her lips would disappear in a tight mean line. She'd start vibrating and humming, and the top of her head would blow off like the lid of a steam kettle, and everything inside would run down her face, melting her until there'd be nothing left but a puddle of Mom stuff. So Bobby told her he was going out, instead.

He let the rusty spring on the screen door have its way as he ran from the kitchen into the Arizona sunshine and summer bug noise, and he was almost out of sight when he heard the satisfying bang! that made all the peacocks scream.

Bobby lazed on down the street, Main Street, the only street, a dirt road really, kicking rocks and looking for devils' horns. Swarms of summertime flies buzzed around his head. He pulled at his jeans and the shorts riding up in the crack of his butt. He kept an eye out for whirlwinds to stand in as he practiced flipping birds, the middle finger of his right hand snicking out like the blade of a switchblade knife.

Do it once, then do it twice, then do it again. This was a necessary man type skill, his cousin fat Edward, who was thirteen and should know, had told him. Necessary for a gee man, Bobby thought (but never said) because that's what he was going to be—a gee man and maybe get himself a good golly molly. Twist and shout! Yes. He flipped off the sky.

And the sky said, "Hey!"

Bobby tipped his head back to see a man in a cage. The cage hung from a high branch of the biggest oak tree around. Jail tree. Everyone called the prisoner Robert; everyone knew he liked to drink whiskey and pinch the bottoms of bar girls. Bobby flipped him off.

Robert held the bars of the cage with both hands and glared down at Bobby. "Don't do that, Bobby B."

"That's not my name," Bobby said and held up his fist and triggered his finger again. Just when his middle finger snapped into position, he jabbed at Robert with his whole hand—a nice bit of style, Bobby thought.

"I told you not to do that!" Robert yelled. He pumped his legs and the cage swung on its rope. Bobby showed him his bird again.

Robert had gotten the cage going around in a circle, and now he crashed it against the trunk of the oak tree. "You just wait till I get out of here!"

Bobby flipped him off again, and then as Robert slumped to the floor of the cage and broke into tears, Bobby ran off down Main Street.

What was it about this gesture, he wondered, that it could make a grown man cry? Such power and magic. It was like when he'd called his cousin Edward a cocksucker, a term he'd gotten from Edward in the first place. Edward had chased him around and around the barn yelling that he'd kill him if he ever got his hands around Bobby's pussy neck. Cats and chickens. It didn't make a lot of sense. There was something potent and dirty about sucking on roosters, but Bobby couldn't figure what it could be. Cock Robin. Or maybe something to do with devil worship; he'd heard they liked to kill things and drink blood, or maybe geeks, the way Edward said they liked to bite the heads off chickens and suck the eggs up through the bleeding top. But wouldn't that make it hensucking?

Bobby discovered a new refinement. As the middle finger of his right hand snicked out, he slapped the whole hand into his left palm, making a sharp smack that scared birds from the rooftops and set a snake to rattling right there in the middle of the road in front of him.

Coiled, pastel pink and blue and orange and green, the duckbill rattlesnake snarled, showing its daffy little needlesharp teeth. It swept its head left and right keeping its bright eyes on Bobby. The snake's dry rattle was so fast, Bobby couldn't see the tail move. He stopped in his tracks and flipped off the snake.

The snake froze like it couldn't believe its eyes then picked up its rattle twice as fast and hard as before. It hissed and spit at Bobby who jumped to the side and jabbed his middle finger into the air, yelled "Yii!" then jumped again. The snake twisted around to follow Bobby who kept moving and yelling and flipping it off. Just as Bobby thought he'd finally gotten the snake to knot itself, a car came barreling out of nowhere and honking its horn like crazy. Bobby jumped out of the way, and the car ran over the snake. Squashed it flat.

"No fair!" Bobby yelled, and when old Mr. Klein poked his head out of the side window to look back and shake his fist at Bobby, Bobby flipped a bird at him.

Mr. Klein braked hard, and the car skidded sideways and crashed into the Bait and Tackle Shop. Bobby hurried on down Main Street.

Mrs. Stokes stood hugging a brown paper bag on the steps of the

Grocery Store. "Don't slouch so, Bobby," she said.

Bobby flipped her off.

Mrs. Stokes collapsed like she'd suddenly been unplugged.

Bobby jerked around like a gun fighter and flipped off the Dime Store, and the store exploded, spewing up electric trains and stuffed animals, comic books and pieces of plastic airplane models.

Bobby flipped off the Bright White Church on the corner, and it jumped into the air then fell onto its side with a splintering crash and the sounds of breaking glass. Flipping fast and furious now, Bobby turned the Little Red Schoolhouse into a big pile of little red bricks.

Bobby flipped off the Court-house, and smoke filled its windows. The mayor ran out screaming, "Fire! Fire!"

Downtown was beginning to look war-torn, worse for wear, maybe tornado-struck.

"You're not being very nice, Bobby," said the West Witch, ugly as sin his father called her, where she sat on the boardwalk with her plastic bag of empty vegetable cans and bits of bright yarn and corked bottles of powders and potions. Bobby flipped her off.

The witch's eyes got big, then she grinned, and Bobby could see she had no teeth. "Maybe you just need something sweet to suck on. A sweet tooth. Or two." She wiggled her eyebrows up and down at him, and sweetness filled his mouth. Chocolate. He backed away, sucking at his teeth. His front teeth. His chocolate teeth, and they were getting smaller fast, dissolving.

The witch sat rocking and slapping her knees and laughing at him, and when he zapped her with the finger again, all he was able to do was knock off her ragged bonnet, and that just seemed to make her laugh harder.

Bobby swallowed the last of his chocolate and ran on down the street, tonguing the space where his top front teeth had been. He stopped in front of the still-standing Hardware Store where he knew there was a mirror in the window. He was so much older now, growing up before his very eyes. He watched in dismay as his new teeth came in. He was a chipmunk. How could he be a gee man if he looked like a big chipmunk? No, a beaver. Bobby the Beaver. There was something about beavers, too, something that put a sly smile on Edward's face. He'd never figure it out in time. You're always a day late and a dollar short, his father liked to say. Bobby flipped off the Hardware Store, reducing it to piles of lumber and nails, tools and electrical parts, pipes and toilet fixtures.

He let his shoulders slump, deliberate bad posture, and slouched on down the smoky street, getting bigger, stumbling into adolescence, feeling mean and shooting I-Meant-To-Do-That! glances around whenever he tripped over his own feet, kicking the town's rubble out of his way, taking time to flip off the county deputy and send his car tumbling with the tumble weeds. Stinking black leather jacket and dirty jeans, torn basketball shoes, flattop, a cool fool, coming up on Molly, the East Witch, as beautiful as the other one was ugly, saying, hey baby. The once-over for this one in her tight purple skirt and lacy white deep-vee blouse, brown and white shoes and bobby sox. Once-over was not enough, so the twice-over. Her dog, a blond Lab, sat by her side giving Bobby the eye, an Elvis sneer on its lips, and a little rumbling growl coming from somewhere deep inside.

"Keep your eyes to yourself, Bobby B," Molly said.

So what could he do but flip her off?

She narrowed her eyes, said, "All right for you, Bobby. You asked for it." She raised an eyebrow.

What was it, he wondered, with these women and their eyebrows? Something pulled his eyes closed, and when he touched his face, he discovered that his eyelashes had grown long and heavy, so long, in fact, that they fell to his chest. He had to take a handful of eyelashes in each hand and pull them up and away from his eyes before he could see Molly standing there smirking with one hand on a cocked hip and a cigarette in the other. She blew a smoky kiss his way.

"I don't suppose you'd let me shine my gee man flashlight in your face?" Bobby asked.

"JC doesn't like that kind of talk, Bobby." She put her hand on the dog's head.

"You named your dog after Jesus Christ?"

"No. After Joseph Campbell."

Like that was his cue, the dog jumped up, circled around young Bobby B, and bit him in the seat of the pants.

Bobby dropped his eyelashes, but he could still see the sudden light. Teen epiphany. He was seized by a sudden need to rip off his clothes, run into the woods, and beat on a drum until his father came down out of the trees.

He turned and shouldered his way through the ragged refugees toward the end of Main Street and the wilderness beyond.

Just outside the remains of town, Edward jumped up from behind a big ocotillo and flipped Bobby off with both hands while doing a shimmy like he had a tail to wag. "Take that, beaver face!" he shouted.

"Same to you!" Bobby grinned and flipped Edward off so hard his cousin's ears were pinned back.

"All right!" Edward slugged Bobby in the shoulder, and the two of them walked on, and as they walked, guys popped up from behind cacti to take potshots with that one finger salute. Snick. Snick. Like a running gun battle, but Bobby and Edward were too fast, and the vanquished soon fell in behind them, and by the time the sun had set, a Society of Men had formed.

They built a fire. They killed and cooked some rabbits. The moon soon gave them the cold shoulder. Coyotes sang. Backslapping, spitting, and farting, the men squatted with their drums in a circle around Bobby, who would soon exclaim sweet gee manly poetry.

REJOICE

The air is so cold and clear and the sea so calm and there, just there, if you shade the arctic sunlight from your eyes, you can see a flat-topped chip off an old iceberg floating in an otherwise empty expanse of blue water, and on the ice a moocow, a huge dog, and two naked white men engaged in Greco-Roman wrestling. Off to one side leaning, a red-lettered sign on a stick in the ice like maybe someone got tired of picketing, says Cease Co.

Mister make the passengers take turns, shoo them from the starboard rails, scatter them like chickens squacking squabbling holding onto their flowered hats and fedoras, waving handkerchiefs, stretching up their necks to look; get them back, I tell you, otherwise they'll tip us, and while you're at it, sound the fog horn, blow the whistle, ring the bells, and come about for a rescue.

Before we could pull them from the ice, one of the combatants leaped onto the cow and rode it into the icy ocean. The other, along with what turned out to be an Irish Wolfhound with unusual front limbs, we were able to get aboard. The rescued man, a Genevese of some education who had most recently traveled to these northern latitudes through the Americas, was soon persuaded to tell his ghoulish tale of reckless creation, unbounded pride, unbearable despair, frustrated revenge, and unfinished business.

The dog he introduced as his faithful assistant and companion, Mucho Poocho. All in good time, he said, when we wondered about the dog's long black evening gloves.

Everything depends on the past, I told her, he said, and we said how true how true and smiled encouragement and made sympathetic noises and put out tentative fingers to touch him lightly on the arm, the head, the back of the ear, the knee, the anus, the navel, the left nostril, go on and on, you're safe now, trust us, be calm, talk.

Blessed be the reanimated, I said, he said, and she said what is this sweet cream of consciousness; this woman, ward of my father and my bride to be, dear Elizabeth who would have to get to know her way around the laboratory and quickly, too, if we were to have any chance of happiness, especially now on the very eve of my great achievement.

I wanted to show her everything. Witness this, I said, yes, give me your hand, touch this machine with all the black knobs and buttons and levers and gauges. Look at all the hoses. Look at the dark hopper. The spark. Watch out! Touch the rough iron crank. Yes, that's it. It hums and hums and pulses. Quite warm, yes. It has taken years of research, years of trial and error, cycle upon cycle of try/fail to bring this machine into existence. So many high hopes dashed.

The immediate ancestor of this machine was a simple reader, a device designed to appreciate Latin utterances which you would enter from a keyboard and which it would display upon a screen. I can see you're wondering how I knew the machine really appreciated the Latin. Well, I would ask it, of course. I would say, for example, so what do you think of ogitocay ergoay umsay? And that most excellent but primitive machine would reply, oh wow that last Classic Latin

Utterance was really something Else!

Proving and providing and paving the way for the current work which shows beyond all doubt that this written record, I slapped the revered volume and dust rose and she sneezed, is composed of such exquisite detail, such esoteric imagery, such private symbolism that it is not simply a book by J, dead all these many years, but rather is J himself!

How can that be, Victor?

It's all here, I said, the whole ball of wax, from soup to nuts, liver and lights, every last scrap, the works, his very essence.

I can bring him back.

This book is a symbolic map of his mind and can be reinstalled now that the proper technology is available.

I've only to pop the book into the hopper here and hook up the hoses and crank the crank and the corpse will dance again darling put out your hand and wake the Finn again.

Oh my, yes, she said, and we said what she said, and he said, so encouraged by this realization, this sudden spacklesparkle in dark eyes, you know we know, I swept the sheet from the body.

You can't imagine the trouble I went through to get the parts. Knocked together from boneyard bits and pieces picked up at the sites of auto accidents, I sewed a lot of it together myself.

Ugg, she said.

Oh, we're not done, I said, we're definitely not done. We still have to idandify the body, I said. Mucho! Bring me the pearls and the red high heels! I pushed at the cheek of the corpse with my finger but it didn't push back. What would you think of a spot of rouge?

Rouge is nice, she said.

And this, I said, and put a small wrapped package next to the body.

What is it?

A mustache.

I peeled back the waxed paper and she leaned in close to look.

So small, she said, one might even say, prissy.

But just the thing, considering the rest of the getup. If it ever gets here. Mucho! There. Just look at how it seems to anchor the nose.

I think you've got it upside down,

Quite right. Look now, isn't that nice?

My assistant ran in with the pearls and shoes, and Elizabeth grabbed my arm and hissed in my ear, my god that dog has hands!

Mucho Poocho is also an early model, I said, he said and reached out a hand to the Wolfhound who snarled and stepped to the rail and stood gazing out at the gray sea.

It's not like you're born knowing how to put bodies together. Feeling a little defensive, and more than a little put out at the hangdog look on Mucho's face, I snatched the red shoes from his hand and fitted them onto the feet of the corpse. The sudden color chased away my irritation and I pulled the head up off the table and draped the string of pearls around the neck.

Next we hook up the hoses, I said.

So in the name of the bladder and of the bones and of the doily moist upon his head, be quiet, Elizabeth, it is not peeing on you, and hold still, that one goes there yes, push, push! Help her Mucho. Our lad's on the way. Hold this now. And this while I crank out a new song for a new age and a new King of the Yeast.

Oh, look, Elizabeth, can't you see the body becoming more inwardly mobile?

I cranked the crank, and the machine chewed pages, and the body moved like a fleshy sack of puppies. Sparks danced from every silvery surface in the lab and our hair stood on end and Mucho Poocho howled a long low Irish howl of lost green days and lost green places.

The body sat up.

Telegram for Mr. Juice!

I knew it, he cried, I knew you couldn't start the melodeum without me, not without me, you wouldn't, you couldn't, not without me. Two thousand and fun! Oh look at all the pretty lights! I explode from the wilderness, your Dudeoronomy daddyo, all dancing shoes and swinging pearls, with a new message to be fluteful and signify! But you want to know about, you say you're just wild about, you say you cannot live without your neither shall, neither shall, neither shall nots. And I say knock it off, cut it out. Cease Co. is talking new rules, a whole new policy. In our winding down, we are winding up. This time the rabbit hole opens into a new century where everyone talks the talk now that Mr. Juice is loose.

He ripped the hoses from his body and swung his legs around to dangle over the edge of the table, and the sun suddenly tossed through the skylight a horseshoe halo around his head, and he pulled at the hoses and dragged the machine to the table and picked it up and threw it across the room where it shattered into twelve inthesink pisces. It'll be better than Dracula's nightout, he said, it'll be wilder than a piece of Mississippi pie from Mr. Chew Chew.

His noodlerumble headnoise, the horrible sound of greaseless wheels turning and turning and turning, shook the walls and made my beakers jitterbug rattled my test tubes my retorts as he rose on jellyjuice legs and spread his arms wide and grinned his fair-weather grin and said what you seize is what you get and said ad albiora alba sanguis agni drink my blood in a cut crystal goblet liberally laced with vodka and stirred with a stalk of fresh celery. He held out a dotted palm and said use this missing period at the very end of things.

He took his first step, then another, monster moving across the scrubbed laboratory floor toward us. Elizabeth took my arm and huddled close. Mucho hid behind us but still peeked around my leg. He'd seen us at once, but now he seemed to be really looking at us and I could see my error written large on his face. Something had gone terribly wrong.

A certain cruel cunning came alive in his eyes, and he questioned me closely, saying, what is that you've got there, my cold mad faery father? He took Elizabeth's arm between a thumb and first finger, very plump, in her slopery slip, my mouseling, little frogchen, touch me with your girlick breath.

I put Elizabeth behind me.

Make me one of those, he said. He could look right over the top of my head and I had no doubt what he meant. I want one of those.

It was easy to see that the experiment had failed. Maybe everything necessary had not been in the book after all, or perhaps my machine had simply failed to extract it all. Or maybe you never know what you'll get until you get it. In any case, I had created an abomination, and now he wanted me to make him a bride.

Never, I said.

Maybe I'll take that one if you won't make me one of my own, he said and lowered his chin and looked up at me like a buffalo calculating a charge.

Leave her alone, I said.

Mink you, Pop.

Oh yeah, well you can just read my mind!

He slapped me to my knees, grabbed me by the shoulders and spun me around and got me around the neck in a wrestling hold from which I had little hope of slipping. Help, I shouted to Mucho Poocho. Attack! Kill! Mucho hunkered down on the floor with a whimper and the monster snortled.

Shall we fiddle with fido?

Not fido, I told him.

Tease fido, eh tease fido, eh eh tease fido.

Mucho put his hands over his eyes, he said, and we all looked at the dog who had been looking back at us over his shoulder but who now looked back out to sea.

It's not my job to make you comfortable, the monster said, and we said maybe he's got a point, lazy poach dogs, the lot of us, and he gave my neck a twist and tossed me to one side.

Perhaps somewhere in his dark semisubconscious he had some feeling for his creator that constrained the twist and left my neck unbroken. Even so I was sorely stunned and quite unable to help Elizabeth who scooted away from the brute in little fits and sneezes.

She avoided him until she reached the wall, then he grabbed her, and she crumbled like a dried flower in his fingers and he looked around in surprise like what happened is that all there is how could she be so fragile this is all so embarrassing.

Birds darkened the skylight and beat the glass with their black wings, thunder sounded, and a cold wind found every crack and stirred my notes, and tossed my hair, and Mr. (call me Cease Co.) Juice blew CEO cigar smoke from his wide nostrils, said we are the Doggymen, and leaped into dance, lifting his knees high happy grape stomping goofy grin, this sad patchwork graveyard doll, celebrating something foul, and dropped to his knees and scrambled bugfast across the room to me, ripping at my clothes, dogcurious nose and doggy lips in the crack of my ass, blew me up justlikethat with smoke and I floated away, a fat macey man balloon belching smoke rings and drifting upright then drifting upside down.

The skylight shattered and black birds like Brimstoker bats swarmed into the lab and settled everywhere, mostly on Elizabeth.

May you have a million years in hell to think about what you've done, I said.

It's the Count who thinks, he said.

I'll have my revenge.

Eat your selfish, he said, it will be cold comfort.

And then he was gone and I swam down to Elizabeth and shooed away the butcherbirds and read the note written on the bottom of her foot: cheep. When had the monster found time to defile the body?

Struck by a sudden suspicion, I sat down on the floor and pulled off my boots. Yes. Notes on the bottoms of both feet. On my left foot, most significantly, a quote from the book itself: I am speaking to us in the second person. On the right foot: Direct quotes from the book will henceforth, both forward and backwards in time, be printed in a holy color that only true believers can see.

So you will agree there was nothing I could have done but hound the monster to the very ends of the earth, and that is what has brought me to these icy wastelands, he said and put his head down on the deck and died like the Easter bunny you've hugged too tightly and we said but hold on a moment, we keep getting the monster and the doctor mixed up. Mucho Poocho spoke then, said, so just who do you think rode the moocow into the sea?

MY MUSTACHE

In lieu of the whiskers which never looked any good anyway—sparse and weedy like someone's neglected strip of lawn on the wrong side of town during a drought and after a yard fire, Lewis superglued a foot-long garter snake to his smooth upper lip. The snake had some trouble adjusting and nipped his face often that first morning, and Lewis was, for probably the first time in his life, thankful he wore glasses, but after a few hours the two of them, snake and man, came to know and love one another. Lewis called the snake My Mustache. He would fed it bugs and baby mice and bird eggs.

Considering his bald head, Lewis figured he'd say things like my hair just slipped down onto my face. Maybe wink and wiggle his eyebrows up and down lewdly.

Ooo la la.

My Mustache would punctuate his points with its forked tongue.

He couldn't wait to show Tess.

Tess didn't like it.

That night, Lewis sat at his kitchen table, absently stroking My

Mustache, eating pitted black olives, tempting the snake with one now and then, chasing away Tess' cigarette smoke with a Queen of England wave, pretending the eruptions in her Spanish eyes didn't really mean anything, making small talk, talking fast and imagining she gave a rat's ass about what he was saying. She'd stare at My Mustache like a hypnotized rabbit then jerk herself erect to shoot him an icy look, then her eyes would be drawn back down to the snake.

"Must you stare, Tess?" Lewis said. "Put out your cigarette and eat your spaghetti. You don't like my marinara?"

Tess jerked her eyes away from the snake. "Lewis," she said. "We have to talk."

"I know that line," Lewis said. "It's what women say just before they show you the door, just before they tell you to hit the road, Jack, and donchoo come back no more no more, donchoo . . ."

"Stop it, Lewis. This is serious."

"I know. I know." Lewis put his hands over his eyes. "I get like this whenever someone special just can't see beyond appearances to the real me." He opened his fingers to peek out at her. "It's not how you look that really counts, Tess."

"Lewis, you have a snake glued to your face!"

"You don't like My Mustache?"

She grabbed her long raven hair with both hands and pulled it away from her head like a tent. "I can't stand this, Lewis. It's always something! This is just one more way you push people away."

"By growing a mustache? You're saying I'm pushing people away by growing a mustache?"

"Ask yourself, Lewis," she said and leaned across the table and put her hand on top of his and squeezed. "Who will want to touch you with a snake glued to your face? You don't want me or anyone else to get too close. That's what the snake is all about."

Lewis looked away, finally pushed into a sulk.

"Just look," she said, not ready to let him withdraw altogether. "Look at the way people are staring at us, at you. Don't you care? Can't you imagine how I feel?"

"Concentrate, Tess," he said. "This is my kitchen. There's no one else here." He pushed the wicker basket of garlic bread in its red checked napkin across the table. "Have some bread."

Tess bit her lip. He thought she would try to convince him again of the reality of the people who followed her everywhere, but she looked down at her hands, then took a deep breath and said, "If there were other people here, Lewis, they'd likely be thinking unkind thoughts about you. And about me for having anything to do with you."

"Screw 'em," Lewis said, deep proletarian indignation emerging and then exploding in his eyes at last. "What made this country great is the way we're different, not the way we're alike."

"This isn't a political question, Lewis."

"Everything is a political question, Tess," he said and snatched up his wine and tossed it at his mouth, splashing Chianti onto My Mustache who hissed and sputtered and spit and fixed Tess with smoldering black snake eyes.

"What?" Tess cocked her head to the side to listen to a voice Lewis couldn't hear. "Yes, I suppose you could be right." She snatched the napkin out of her lap and tossed it onto the table and got to her feet. "We've agreed, Lewis. All of us. We can't have anything more to do with you until you get some help."

He watched her walk for the door, watched her long legs, listened to her heels click on his polished hardwood floor, watched the way her red and green checked skirt swayed first this way and then that way, saw the sad look she gave him over one shoulder as she reached for the brass doorknob, saying, "I guess we'll all just leave you alone, Lewis."

"Wait!" Lewis pushed up from the table, trotted across the room, came up behind her, and put his arms around her waist and pulled her close. "Don't leave, Tess." He kissed her ear. My Mustache stretched its head around and looked her in the eye.

Tess screamed and elbowed him in the ribs.

He couldn't let her leave. If he let her go now, she'd be out the door and out of his life, probably forever. He tossed her toward the couch and moved in front of the door and spread his legs and opened his arms over his head, transforming himself into a giant X to block her exit.

"Oh, Lewis." Her tone was so sad and disappointed.

He dropped his arms and moved away from the door. He couldn't force her to stay. Now was the time for innovative action.

"I'll shave!" he cried and dashed for the bathroom. "Don't leave!"

Tess looked around the room. "Okay," she said. "Once more. Just one more time." She straightened her clothes and crossed her legs and settled back on the couch to watch the bathroom door.

Lewis was a long time in there banging around and running the faucets and finally flushing the toilet. When he emerged, he'd put on a big smile below what might have been mistaken for a milk mustache.

Tess gasped.

"It's the Band-Aid isn't it?" Lewis touched the white strip under his nose. "Well, it'll take some time for the ah . . . residue of My Mustache to wear off."

Tess couldn't tear her eyes away from the creature glued to Lewis' bald head. The turtle clawed at the air, moving all four legs and stretching out its neck as if it were swimming to Bermuda, but it wasn't going anywhere.

"What?" Lewis said. "What?" He patted the turtle. "My New Hairpiece? You don't like it. Is there no pleasing you, Tess?"

WE KILL A BICYCLE

We've hidden ourselves along the bike path. Everything is so green and wet and restless, rustling with the river breeze. Ants keep getting on my arms, but I flick them off with my fingers and imagine their tiny screams as they shoot through the air and fall and fall into the moldy leaves around my knees. Laura is out there somewhere. I want to put my tongue in her ear. I want to hear her suck in her breath when I do it. I want to make her smile. She's so serious these days, so far away, somehow.

What I hear instead is Rodney whispering. I want to tell him to knock it off, but I know it wouldn't do any good. He's into one of his stories about the old days, about killing skateboards, easy meat, and I want to say to him, Rodney, I want to say, so if they were such good eating and if they were so silly, like the way you could hear them a long way off trying to get up on some curb or low concrete wall for no reason a person could figure out, and if they were so easy to catch the way you make them sound, what I want to know is why you old farts killed them all. How come you didn't leave any for us? None of you could have been that hungry. Why didn't you think of your grandchildren?

All of us are hungry now. Old folks to babies. I dig through the leaves around my knees and find a slick stone and toss it into the brush from which comes Rodney's voice, and he says ouch! and then some other nasty stuff, he's worse than the children, but then we all hear the treetop scout whistle, bicycles coming, and even Rodney gets quiet. I can smell my own excitement, peppery sweat, and I rub my wet palms up and down over the hair on my thighs. We don't get bikes every day.

We've hidden ourselves just inside a long green corridor of trees and thick brush. There is a small rise in the grassy stretch of ground before the bike path enters the forest, and I now see a bike pull up and stop. No other bikes come up beside her, and I wonder if maybe I should be not believing our luck. Can she really be alone? She puts a hand above her eyes to shade the late afternoon sun. She pulls her shoulders up, and I see her tanned breasts rise, then she lets her shoulders drop. She looks behind, then peers into our leafy corridor again. She's going to chance it. I know she is. Sometimes I have a feeling for these things.

She puts her hands on her handlebars and moves back and forth like she's winding up to make a run for it. Then she's rolling right at us, pedaling for all she's worth, white thighs pumping, long gold hair flowing out behind her.

Once she gets into our corridor, a couple of us, I don't look to see who, probably Magdalen and Holly, step out to block any retreat she might make. I get ready to jump. Laura has insisted on being the blocker for days now, but this is the first time we've had a bike for her to actually block. It's like she's got something to prove. She doesn't know that I always put big Sidney up ahead of her in case the bike gets by her.

I see Laura step out in front of the bike. No way a bicycle would stop for a person as small and fine-boned as my Laura, Laura with her black tangled hair and her dirty feet, but she jumps up and down and waves her hands in the air and makes a lot of scary noises, and it's enough to make the bike swerve to the side, and that's just when I jump out and deliver the soles of my feet to the bike's upper body and the side of her head, and she goes tumbling, and the rest of our group is on her, everyone with a shout and a stick, everyone whooping and swatting the life out of what will be our lunch and dinner, too, maybe even some left over for tomorrow. Everyone participates. We make no apologies. No one is allowed to be squeamish; if you want to eat it, you've got to be willing to kill it. I shoulder my way in for a few licks of my own. It doesn't take long to kill the bicycle. She doesn't put up much of a fight.

I move everyone back, and I pull the bicycle's legs up over her handlebars and then up to her chest so I can get at her tailbone where the metal parts join the meat parts. I run my fingers up that shaft until I find just the right place where metal becomes bone. I put my hand out for the bolt cutters. Someone takes the bike by the arms and legs and applies light pressure, and I put the bolt cutters on the place I've located. I've gotten it right. The cutters snip through the shaft easily with a satisfying crunch.

I carry the bolt cutters over my shoulder as I follow the People dragging the meat back toward camp. I get way down the green corridor before something makes me look back at the metal parts of the bike. What I see freezes me inside. Laura is just standing there looking down at the metal parts, but it's something about the way she's standing that frightens me. She nudges the front wheel with her foot, then she bends down and picks up the horrid thing and sets it on its wheels.

"Laura!" I shout.

She looks up at me, and I imagine she's already got the look of a startled bike in her eyes. I run toward her.

She quickly swings onto the machine, and I groan. I see her tremble from head to toe as the merging happens. She squeezes her eyes closed, and her tongue pokes out of her mouth.

Just before I can grab her (not that I would know what to do with her now anyway) she screams and her eyes go wide and she wheels around and pedals for the grasslands. She still hasn't figured out how to get her tongue back into her mouth. I run after her, but a person can't outrun a bicycle.

I run some, following, then I walk. I lose sight of her, then I see her again. This following feels entirely fruitless, but I can't stop. I know she's gone, but that fact hasn't yet hit me down low where I live. Soon though, I see Laura join a herd of bikes congregating on a small grassy hill. The big male wheels up and lightly touches her breasts then nuzzles her ear. They look so good together, like centaurs. I want to kill him. I walk to the foot of the hill.

The bikes watch me closely, but they don't move off. They know I am no danger to them out here. In fact, if I keep walking, there is a good chance they could be danger to me. I stop.

"Laura," I call. "How can you do this? What about us?"

She pushes away from the big male and wheels around in a circle then comes down the hill a little until I can see her eyes. He watches her closely but doesn't try to stop her, poised as he is pointing down the hill at me with one foot on the ground the other on a pedal, his hands on his hips, ready, I guess, to rescue her if I try anything funny. The rest of the herd titters nervously behind him.

"I want the wind, Desmond," she says.

"The wind?"

Her look destroys me. She doesn't see me at all. She wheels around, and the bikes make way for her as she moves up the hill. She gives me one last glance back over her shoulder. I don't follow.

The wind? I have been abandoned by a woman who wants the wind. What can that mean? It makes me crazy. I want to kill something, and I'm not even hungry.

Okay, I've snapped. That's the way it is, and if that's the way it is, maybe I'll go out and do something daring, maybe do something a little foolish, maybe do something that will show what I'm made of.

Maybe I'll go down into the streets and kill myself a car.

Or die trying.

Be a hero.

Get slapped on the butt by the guys.

Listen to the crowd roar.

Get the girl back.

Be happy.

Sure.

A HOLIDAY JUNKET

So we teleport for the holidays to a world where everyone is required to carry a huge fishbowl all of the time. It takes both hands to hold the heavy bowl, and once you're holding it, there's no way to let go. The fish in the bowl is a barking goldfish. It likes to eat spiders. The so-called kamikaze spider is as big as a basketball, and it always goes for your face. Once you have a spider trying to suck out your eyes, you have very little time to perform the only course of action open to you. What you must do is plunge your head into the bowl so your barking goldfish can eat the kamikaze spider. None of this was explained in the brochure.

Also big news to us is the fact that this is a world where the dimension necessary for long distance telepathy is missing. Just as sound cannot cross a vacuum, here thoughts do not travel in the ether. I could beam my intentions at her until I was blue in the face, and it wouldn't do any good.

What we must do is somehow touch heads. If we can touch heads I can ask her if maybe we shouldn't get out of here. If she agrees, and

I can't imagine that she won't, we can hotfoot it through the forest and across the creek to the exit portal which if I'm not mistaken I can actually see from here. Touching heads, however, is going to be a big problem, since we're both holding these really big fishbowls.

The sky is sea green, and the puffy pink clouds racing across it move too quickly to really be clouds, not that I thought there were clouds in the first place, since we came to know everything we needed to know about this world as soon as we popped into existence here. None of it makes me feel like singing Christmas carols.

I suppose I could just take off running. Would she get the idea and follow? Or would she misunderstand and think that I'd known what this world was like all along and that I'd lured her here to abandon her?

I cluck my tongue at her trying to get her attention so she'll come over here so maybe we can touch heads, but she's looking around fearfully like something might jump out of the feather duster trees and grab her, and the look on her face would be funny and adorable, oh you silly goose, if it were not the case that her fears are entirely justified. Even the little bugs on this world are as big as your feet.

She finally sees me making faces at her and comes over and our fishbowls clink together as we try to go head to head. Our fish thrash around barking like crazy and snapping at each other through the glass. Whenever we lean in to touch, the fish leap up out of the water and nip at our chins. Boy, if I ever do manage to get a thought in edgewise what I'll think is maybe we should have opted for a more traditional holiday with growling mall crowds and a rented uncle albert singing drunken sailor songs and fruit cake and santa clauses and colored lights and disappointed children and eggnog.

I walk around her hoping we can touch from the rear, but as it turns out, and this is not something I'd realized earlier, our butts are almost perfectly matched height-wise. And the bowls are so heavy. I can't lean far enough back to touch my head to hers without spilling water out of my fishbowl, and if I spilled too much water and the fish got stressed and became maybe moody and lethargic, who would eat the kamikaze spider surely even now tensing for a leap at my face?

I feel a sudden flash of irritation, and I'm glad we didn't connect just then. Otherwise we might have exchanged unkind remarks about our respective butts.

I move to her side but no matter how we arrange ourselves we cannot connect. Front to back? No good. All we do is produce a clinking clanking splashing and barking cacophony of goldfish.

Our struggle to re-establish the connection we have always had suddenly becomes desperate as I realize, and I can see it in her eyes that it has dawned upon her too, that we may never hook up again. We could be stranded and alone like this forever. We spend a couple of minutes jumping around making hopeless and helpless hooting sounds, grunts and cries, whimpers and finally barks not too different from the barks of our goldfish.

Then there is a quiet moment. The eye of the storm. And then we panic. I can't see her fishbowl; I can only see her. She fills my vision, and nothing matters as much as our reunion. I cannot rationally appraise the danger we face as we rush together and meet like belly-bumping cowboys and our bowls shatter and our fish fall into the high grass, and she wet, slippery and shivering rushes into my arms.

There is a momentary riot of chewing sounds from the grass, and then the worldwide bug symphony that I'd scarcely noticed before stops absolutely. The pink non-clouds gather above us like a fastforward weather report. Those black drops dropping will probably be spiders.

I pull her in close and we touch heads, and in an explosion of color and big bands, jungle orchids and satin cat feet up and down my spine, it's like a big part of your mind has just wondered off whistling, and now it's back and all the pieces snap into place, a cosmic ah ha and she me we spiral down and down to a perfect state of not quite seamless sameness, the two of us, the one of us. You can phone your congressperson, and you can write a letter to the editor. You can curse your luck, and you can shake your fist at the sky. You can drop to your knees in an eleventh hour appeal to magic. But in the end there is really only this.

We make a dash for it.

GIANT STEP

Gregory figured the young policeman would hit him tonight, because at some deep level the policeman knew that, but for the grace of God and the fact that people still paid taxes for prisons and the personnel to put and keep other people in prisons, he might be homeless and living in a space suit just like Gregory. Just a paycheck away and frightened, with pale blue angry eyes and a goofy cowlick, he probably had a pretty young wife who sent him off to work with a kiss and a tuna fish sandwich wrapped in waxed paper, maybe the same waxed paper that blew across the rainbow oil slick in the gutter puddle by Gregory's feet.

In a sudden flash of inspiration, Gregory knew what to say to him. "Well, Officer," he shouted through his helmet, "we can't move along, because all motion is impossible. Zeno proved that thousands of years ago."

Nancy, also suited and sitting on the sidewalk beside Gregory, touched helmets with him. "Is that logic I smell?"

Her seven-year-old granddaughter Kim stood behind her. Kim's parents had died years ago in the food riots. Like the god of Amos, the government still guaranteed the people clean teeth. Kim hung out with Nancy and didn't talk much these days. She wore a silvery suit sized down for the temporally challenged, and tonight she tapped the side of her helmet with a white plastic spoon and stared up into the sky.

Silver-suited figures of all sizes moved in and out of the street shadows, dodging sluggish honking cars and trucks, and flickering with neon when they passed under the signs of surviving merchants. The suits had toilet functions, heating and cooling units, rechargeable batteries, water bottles, and air tanks, all the comforts of home. Best of all, supporters of the plan privately claimed, once you sealed a wino up in a space suit, you couldn't smell him. At curfew you could pile the people up like cordwood. But hey, skeptics had cried, surely there can't be enough space suits for what amounts to maybe a third of the population. No problem. We make more suits, put all those guys who lost their jobs when we canceled the space program back to work.

The young policeman squatted down in front of Gregory. He unhooked his big flashlight and shined it in Gregory's face for a few moments. Then he put the flashlight away. Maybe he had more curiosity than most, Gregory thought, maybe if the universities had still been funded, he could have been a passable student. Maybe he wouldn't hit Gregory, after all.

"So what's the story on this Zeno guy, Professor?"

"Yes, tell us, Oh Wise One," Nancy said. "How is it that all motion is impossible?" Nancy was an out-of-work English professor and tended to scoff at all things scientific. She pulled Kim around and down on her lap and wrapped an arm around the child. There weren't many stars to see through the smoggy city lights, but at least one of them captured Kim's attention. She settled back and stared up at the night sky.

"Well, suppose you want to move from here to, say, Mr. Wilson's store." Gregory pointed at the small grocery occupying the bottom floor of an otherwise gutted building at the end of the block. "To do that, surely you'll admit you'd have to go through a point that is halfway between here and there. Say, that big pile of steaming garbage in front of the gun shop. Where the dogs are?"

"Yeah. So?" the policeman said.

"Well, to get to the pile of steaming garbage, Officer, surely you can see you'd first have to go through some point that is halfway between here and the garbage, say that broken fire hydrant."

"Yeah, okay, first I walk to the fire hydrant, then I walk to the garbage, then I walk to Wilson's store. So what's the problem?"

"But to get to the fire hydrant, you'd have to walk through a point that is halfway between here and the fire hydrant. Right?"

"I suppose."

"But to get to that point, you'd have to walk to a point that's halfway between those two points, and to get to that point you'd have to walk to a point that was halfway between those two points, and so on and so on."

The policeman didn't look happy, and Gregory thought maybe he'd made a big mistake talking about Zeno. What if paradoxes pissed off the police? Gregory pushed on anyway. What else could he do? Just go silent?

"No matter how small the distance, Officer, you still have to first move through the halfway point. So, not only can you not move from here to Mr. Wilson's store, you can't move away from here at all. And that's why we can't move along."

"I think maybe I'll bonk you with my stick, Professor," the policeman said.

"But it wouldn't be a real bonk, would it, Officer?" Nancy asked. She reached out and patted the policeman's knee. Nancy, tough as

179

nails in the old days, a deconstructor of Brontës and cooker of fiery curries, had nonetheless taken instruction from the streets and could now do a respectable grandmother whenever the occasion demanded.

"What do you mean, Nancy?" Gregory sounded nervous and he kept an eye on the policeman's nightstick.

"Well," Nancy said, still smiling at the young policeman, "if motion is impossible, yet we still perceive motion, it must mean that we are deceived. What we see is an illusion. If the officer hits you with his stick, you'll only think it hurts."

"Idealism," Gregory said, making the word sound like another name for utter nonsense.

"Exactly," Nancy said. "And since all material matters are illusions, we can, in fact, move along as this nice young man has suggested we do by simply imagining ourselves elsewhere."

"You are at least half right," Gregory said. "There is a way out of this conundrum. The answer requires no mysticism, however. It's just simple materialism. Imagine we've cut our distance down until it is very very small." Gregory took a nail from his utility pouch and scratched a line in the sidewalk.

$$X\rule{3cm}{0.4pt}Y\rule{3cm}{0.4pt}Z$$

"The space between X and Z is the first tiny, tiny distance you must move before you can move on through the rest of the halves and finally get from here to Mr. Wilson's store," Gregory said.

"Seems pretty big to me," the policeman said.

"It's a diagram!" Gregory heard the irritation in his voice and added in a softer tone, "It's blown up."

"Oh," the policeman said. "I suppose you'll say we have to move through Y to get to Z, and you'll start this whole stupid business all over again."

"No," Gregory said. "That's my point. At some very small scale, there is a point where we move from X to Z in one discrete step without going through Y. That's what makes motion possible. We move in tiny little steps. We sort of putt-putt along through, well, hyperspace, for lack of a better word."

"I'm sure glad you got rid of the mysticism, Gregory," Nancy said, "but your putt-putting along will be a little slow for the officer, I think. In my scheme, we can move long distances very quickly."

"I don't see why, in principle, we cannot move long distances in my scheme, too," Gregory said. "If you can move a small discrete step without passing through any intermediate points, I don't see why you can't move a large distance in a single step."

"Look out!" Kim cried.

Nancy grabbed his hand, and Gregory looked up in time to see the policeman's nightstick coming down at his face.

Before the stick could crack his faceplate, the policeman disappeared. In fact, the whole street disappeared. Gregory, Nancy, and Kim popped back into existence overlooking a dry red river valley. The empty red rolling vista went on and on forever. Red sand beneath their boots. Red dust blowing everywhere. Funny-looking daytime sky. No bushes. No birds.

"So much room!" Kim stretched out her arms and skipped around in a circle.

"Where are we?" Nancy shouted through her helmet.

"Mars, I think," Gregory said. "Well, I hope the implosion at least knocked the cop over."

"Maybe you convinced him," Nancy said. "Maybe he's realized that all motion is impossible and he's just sitting there with that silly stick of his. In any case, you can see I was right. Idealism wins the day."

"Materialism," Gregory said. "The evidence is clear."

"You're both wrong," Kim cried. "I did it!"

Gregory grabbed her shoulders and stopped her dancing. He bent over her and touched his faceplate to hers.

Nancy leaned in, helmet to helmet, too. "And just how did you do that, young lady?"

"Yes, tell us," Gregory said.

"I wish I may, I wish I might," Kim said.

QUITE CONTRARY

In those days, I was a big, bearded, bald guy with an ax, grinding down the boulevard in my '57 Chevy, looking for something pretty to chop.

These days, a woman who calls me Mary feeds me chocolate chip cookies as I snuggle on the lap of the man who calls me Kitten. The man has his hand on my thigh. We watch TV. I know I've got a milk mustache. I know it looks cute. It's Howdy Doody time.

Back then Alfonso says to me, "Louie." He says, "Louie." He says, "Louie Lew Eye, you wanna go looking for pussy?"

I say I sure do, and Alfonso's so happy he crushes his beer can on his forehead. We pile into the Chevy and cruise the dark dream city, through the canyons of slick black towers, whistling at the chocolate chicks, the valley vanilla in hot pants, going oh baby, oh mama, have I got something for you. Whoop, whoop.

These people, these Capeks, Mommy and Daddy. She knows he's got his hand on my thigh, but she's pretending she doesn't, rushing in with the cookies, talking too loud, pushing at her goofy boo font hair

183

do, looking everywhere but down at my leg and his hand, rushing out again to bang some pots and pans together, coming back. He knows she knows, and that's what gets him off. The way he never takes his hard eyes off her as she moves, the sweat beading on his naked upper lip, his whole body whispering look look just look at what I'm doing I dare you to look. I've decided it doesn't have much to do with me. I bet if I lifted my hip a little and gave him a good squeeze between the legs, he'd toss me right into Buffalo Bob's face.

That night, me and Alfonso see this Sally Capek chick he knows from the office where he sweeps up. What's she doing down here this time of night? He doesn't know. I don't care. I got beer and I got my ax and it's summertime and the living is easy. She's got long legs, and I love the way she marches into the parking lot, looking neither left nor right, hugging her purse to her breasts. Nervous, yes. I like that. She gets into a white Oldsmobile, and I hang back a little so she won't know I'm on her tail.

She's back again. "More milk? More milk?"

The man does a thing he's been doing a lot lately. He takes my chin in his hand and turns my head so he can study my face closely like he's cataloging all the ways I don't look like him. He only does that when she's there to see it.

I remember Mama.

Alfonso's sitting on the ground with his back to the left front tire of her Oldsmobile, my ax in his head, his crotch all dark where he's pissed himself. Crazy Alfonso. He should have known that when I say me first, I mean me first. I'm done now and he could have taken his turn before I let my ax have her, but, no, he's got to give me lip. I look down at the Capek chick where she's whimpering and sniffling, all white ass and crouched in the back seat, and she leaps into my face with something bright, something sharp, and I'm standing in my room, dolls and stuffed animals and pink walls, pink bed, pink light from a pink lamp on a tiny pink dressing table covered with pink bottles. It's like the inside of Barbie's snatch. I smell like I just got out of a bubble bath. What's this? What's this? I run my hands down my boyish chest and finger my tight little twat. So strange.

I look and I listen. I creep around at night after they've tucked me in and kissed me on the nose. I know what they do. I know what they say. They don't know that I know. They say stupid stuff like "Little pitchers have big ears." Shush, shush.

Things are coming to a boil. The man reaches forward and clicks off the TV, sets me on my feet, says, "Why don't you run along and play in your room, Kitten." The woman's got her arms folded. Her lips are tight and white. She taps her foot on the floor.

I've got a lovely bunch of garden tools under my bed. I spend some time laying them out on the floor, long hedge clippers, darling little hand-held rake, a sharp spade, other stuff, then I spend some time operating on the surviving dolls and stuffed animals. Snip, snip.

I probably couldn't lift an ax even if I could find one, but I've got a cute little hatchet. I call him Mr. Chopper.

"'Lo, Mr. Chopper," I say.

"Let's swing, Mary."

I put Mr. Chopper's cool, cool blade to my lips, and a shudder of pleasure shakes me right down to my pink painted toe nails.

"Louie Louie," I whisper.

Daddy's turned on a ball game of some kind. I can hear the crowd roar. He's scrunched down in his chair, and I can just see the top of his head. I come up behind and lift Mr. Chopper high above my head.

"Whoosh!" says Mr. Chopper, and the blood flows and Daddy howls.

One whack isn't enough, so I give him another. Mommy runs in.

She looks like she's going to scream, but I see, too, she's doing her sums, putting two and two together, calculating, like that night in the back seat of her Oldsmobile. She'll be better off without him. This is something she's wanted to do herself.

"Hey Mama," I say all low and sexy. I chuckle at the way her eyes go wide when she recognizes my voice.

Doing Time

We congregate in the weeds and broken bottles of the vacant lot across from the court-house this summer evening, and I whip my cadre of hardcore troops into a revolutionary frenzy.

We build a big fire of rotten boards and old tires. A crowd gathers. We circle the fire, chanting uplifting slogans and waving tiny American flags. We toss the flags in the fire. A fight breaks out.

A riot squad fills the air with tear gas and rubber bullets, and before I can slip away, a chubby man with rosy cheeks, a neat brown suit, and a .357 Magnum tells me his name is Special Officer Mallory. He wants me to put up my hands.

My trial is speedy and mostly by phone. I'm sentenced to five years, and I spend it locked up in a shed behind a classic ranch house on Willow Street. A guy named Louie owns the house. He's picked up my contract.

Louie likes to hose me off before meals. What that means is he pulls out his shriveled pink dong and pees all over me where I'm tied to a folding metal cot.

"You stupid son of a bitch, Louie," I tell him. "Don't you know you'll be the prisoner some day? Everyone slips up. You never know. I just might pick up your contract, next time."

"Oh, no, John." He shivers dramatically. "Wouldn't that be terrible!" If Louie had a tail he'd be wagging it. Stupid son of a bitch. Food's good though, and Louie takes me out on a long rope every day to play in the yard. Could be worse.

Louie cries real tears when they make him let me go.

So what I do after leaving Louie is photograph the flag and make about a dozen copies on the machine in the court-house. A bunch of people see me do that. I've got an attitude, and I'm getting a bad reputation. Someone tips off Mallory and he's in the crowd a little later, around my fire, where I burn the copies of the photograph of the flag. Confusion ripples through the crowd. People step forward; people step back. They can't decide if this is sufficient provocation for a riot. Finally, though, someone takes the initiative and throws a punch. One thing leads to another. Cars get tipped over; windows get broken; stores get looted. I get arrested. Mallory takes care of that personally.

I spend three days handcuffed to the door of his car while the Supreme Court, our legacy of the Reagan Bush Quayle Bush years, deliberates. They decide burning any likeness of the flag is covered by the law. I spend seven years chained to a shopping cart following a derelict named Bob around the city, there being by this time more prisoners than foster guards with buildings. Bob, who shuffles along with enough room in his baggy pants for an extra butt, mostly ignores me as he pushes his cart from place to place, and much as I hate to say it, I miss Louie. At least he talked to me. We sleep in doorways. The money Bob gets for me buys him a steady supply of fortified wine but not much food. I lose a lot of weight.

When my time is up, I bully Bob into pushing us down to the police station where they let me go. "I hope you learned your lesson," the desk sergeant says.

Sure. What I do is get a red marking pen and tear a white bed sheet into flag size and write the words "US flag" on it. Then I burn it. Since I'm TV news by now, the violence is truly spectacular. The underclass neighborhoods, that is to say, maybe ninety percent of the city, are alive with the sound of gunfire, alight with fierce fires gleaming in broken glass. Cars like toppled dead bugs litter the streets.

From the look on Mallory's face, I can tell I'm beginning to piss him off. He drags me into the basement of police headquarters and turns me over to a man in a dirty white lab coat who tells me his name is Dr. Paul. Dr. Paul wants me to take the newly legislated Good Citizen Test. I'd been hoping to avoid that.

I tell him to hide his test in a dark and smelly, but extremely personal, place.

"I'm authorized to shoot you for being uncooperative during the test," he says.

"And what if I take the test, and you decide I'm a socialist or that I have homosexual tendencies or that I can read or something?"

"Then I'm authorized to shoot you," he says.

Just to see what happens, I tell Dr. Paul what it feels like to burn a flag.

"Ah, ha!" He jumps up and whips out a recorder he's had hidden under his greasy coat. "That'll cost you another five years!"

He finally gets his breathing under control and calms down enough to read me the questions on the Good Citizen Test. What I do is pretend I'm Mallory as I answer the questions. I just keep asking myself, "How would Special Officer Mallory answer this question?"

I pass the test. That doesn't please Mallory, who gets really steamed and red in the face, but then Dr. Paul gives him the tape, and that cheers him up.

The Judge is in full agreement that five years ought to be tacked onto my latest sentence—five years for causing an uncooperative idea to become lodged in another citizen's mind.

Mallory asks to pick up my contract himself, saying that since he's arrested me so many times for basically the same crime, my former jailers must not have properly applied all available modern rehabilitation techniques. He wants a shot at it himself. Sounds like a good idea to me, says the Judge. So I go home with Mallory.

A cockroach is doing enthusiastic pushups on my nose. Being chained to the clammy, cold dungeon wall of Mallory's basement, I can't do much about it.

Turns out I'm not Mallory's only prisoner. I shouldn't be surprised, what with maybe half the population at any given time being prisoners. Her name is Connie.

"So whatcha in for, Connie?"

"Missing church too many Sundays in a row," she says.

I've never been locked up with a woman before. In fact, it occurs to me that it's been years and years since I spent any time at all with a woman. She's skinny with ragged blond hair, and she's pretty grimy. Early thirties, I guess. I think she's beautiful. Heaven, I decide, is being locked up in a small airless place with a dirty woman.

Nothing's ever perfect, though. We strain against our chains and whisper all the nasty things we'd do to one another if we could touch. I wonder if all these years of confinement could be doing something to my basic human dignity.

Oh, Connie!

I'm in love.

A couple of days later she asks me, "So what are you thinking, John?"

I tell her I'm visualizing burning the Stars and Stripes.

The door bursts open and Mallory rushes in. "I heard that! I heard that!" he shouts. "This'll be life, John. At long last, I'll take you off the streets for good."

I resent his interruption. "You can't get me for just visualizing it, Mallory," I say.

"No? Hold that thought." Mallory dials his portable phone. "Get me the Supreme Court," he says and listens. I can see him nodding and hear him muttering, and a few minutes later, he jams down the phone antenna. "Turns out I can."

Doesn't matter too much, I decide. I'll spend the years smelling Connie.

But Mallory unchains her, helps her stand. "Nice work, Sergeant," he tells her.

She gives me a mean smile and calls me an old fart.

They leave me alone in the dark.

I get real discouraged, and I wonder if maybe I'm just pissing into the wind.

THE NEXT BEST THING

You've got to discipline your tattoos regularly. Otherwise, they get lazy or uppity—one or the other. I'd set aside the afternoon before Christmas for that purpose, and I was drinking beer and sneaking up on the screaming eagle under my left arm when someone tapped on my door. I put on my mild-mannered-account-executive persona, pulled on my pants and got into my bathrobe.

When I opened the door, I saw Deborah standing there looking good in jeans and western checked shirt, blond hair tied up in a ponytail. Yes, good but sad, too, since it had only been I forget how many days since Tim died.

"I need your help," she said.

I groaned. This had to be about Tim's last request. Everyone knew what he expected his friends to do should he be cruelly snatched away by Death.

"Come on, Deborah," I said. "They'll never let you have him." I was already making up excuses, because I figured what she probably wanted was help stealing his body from the funeral home.

"Oh, that," she said. "He's already in the trunk of my car."

I had met Deborah and Tim at a motivation seminar in Florida several years before. He was the cadaverous ex-astronaut (so the story went) and she was his sci-fi sweetie. Our two worlds were quite different but they seemed to compliment one another pretty well. We became fast friends, a threesome, sometimes a foursome, usually a threesome, so when she looked at me with those deep brown eyes and said, come on I really really really do need you, I changed my clothes and we went.

Tim's last wish had been that his remains be shot into space. I didn't think there was much danger we'd be doing that this rainy afternoon.

Deborah drove well, if a little too fast, out of town and into the Oregon countryside on a road I knew led nowhere but farm country. What could she have in mind?

"The downside to death," she said, "is that it's the last thing you'll ever do."

I waited for her to fill me in on the upside.

"The upside," she said, "is that you do that one last thing forever."

I thought she had it backwards, but I didn't say so.

Deborah, Deborah.

I wondered how she'd gotten Tim's long body into the truck of her car. Weren't dead people supposed to be stiff? She'd waltzed Tim out of the funeral home right under the noses of whoever was holding down the fort the day before Christmas. She was easy to underestimate. You might, for example, get stinking drunk one night when Tim was out of town and call her Debby, maybe even complain that Debby Does Diddly, but you'd only do it once. She was a woman with edges so sharp you even dream about them, you wake up bleeding.

"Will you pay attention?" she said. I realized she'd been talking to me for some time. "Here. We're coming up on it now."

Up ahead was a big white sign—billboard size. I couldn't make it out. Words. A picture. We got closer. I still couldn't make it out. We stopped. "You'll have to open the gate," she said.

I got out and looked up at the sign. It said, "Manvil The Magnificent! Big Breasted Birds." The picture was a happy hayseed hooking a thumb over his shoulder at a grinning steroid turkey.

"Up here a ways," she said when I got back in the car, "we'll have to be very, very quiet."

"Why? Are we hunting wabbits?"

She rolled her eyes at me.

The road snaked through deep forest for a while, and then I could see light ahead indicating we would soon be breaking into the open, but before we got there, Deborah turned off the main road. We slowly skirted the edge of the forest until she found what she was looking for. When we came out of the trees, there was a small hill, little more than a bump, in the middle of a field of what must have once been corn. On top of the hill was a smokestack.

Deborah turned off the engine. "The house," she whispered, "is only a few hundred yards beyond the hill. We'll need to be careful."

I assumed she meant the house of the magnificent turkey farmer, Manvil. She got out of the car and closed the door carefully. Then she eased open the back door and nodded me over. "Help me unload."

I helped her carry boxes and rope and things I couldn't identify up the hill. Something about the smokestack pulled at my mind. I almost had it as I set down each load and turned to go back for another. When we'd unloaded everything and I was taking a moment near the top of the hill to catch my breath, the pieces fell into place.

That was no smokestack!

It was a big gun. A cannon, in fact, but hugely exaggerated like something you'd see in a circus.

RAY VUKCEVICH

"Now we wait for dark," Deborah said. "Come on, let's crawl up by the cannon and take a look at the house."

We moved up on the circus cannon but dropped to our knees before we reached it. I could see it had once been painted red, white, and blue. Now it was rusting in a corn field. Near the top of the hill we got down on our bellies and crawled up and looked over.

In the meadow below there was a farmhouse, a red barn, and a white silo. Set away from those buildings were several sheds surrounded by chicken-wire fences. There were many turkeys in the pens, so many turkeys I wondered if Manvil the Magnificent had sold any at all this holiday season.

Everything was a lot closer than I'd expected.

Deborah scanned the scene through a pair of powerful binoculars.

"There's something seriously wrong with those turkeys." She handed me the binoculars.

I studied the turkeys. They did seem to be bigger and bustier than I remembered turkeys being, but I couldn't see anything to worry about. "What do you mean?" I asked.

"Are you blind?" She gave me a look. "They have arms. Obviously Manvil has reached back in time somehow and crossed his turkeys with their ancient ancestors. In his drive to minimize wing and maximize breast, he has turned them into creatures half modern table bird and half ancient dinosaur. T-rex would be my guess."

I looked again. No arms. This was just another example of what happened when our two very different worlds touched but didn't exactly mesh.

Or maybe she was just yanking my chain.

"Oh, yeah," I said. "Arms."

"Our window will be very small," she said. "We'll have to wait until it's just dark enough that they won't see us unless they're looking right at us, but not so dark we can't see what we're doing."

196

"How will we know?" I asked.

"Look," she said. "You can see into the living room. When they turn on the Christmas tree, conditions should be optimal."

I looked through the binoculars again. Yes, I could see the Christmas tree. And a woman in an apron. She seemed to be talking to someone I couldn't see, probably a child down under the tree where the presents would be.

A man with a huge handlebar mustache came up behind the woman and put his hands on her shoulders. A moment later the Christmas tree lights came on, and a small girl poked her head up, smiling.

Deborah rolled over on her back. "Can you get him?" She didn't look at me when she asked it. "I'll prepare the cannon."

"What do you know about cannons, Deborah?"

"I looked it up," she said. "I know what to do." She did look at me then, just looked, just waited. She'd already told me what she wanted me to do.

Finally I couldn't stand it. "Okay," I said, "give me the car keys."

I wrestled Tim out of the car. He didn't really have much of a smell. They probably did something about that at the funeral home. Nevertheless the thought of how he should smell threatened to make me vomit frogs. It was the idea of it. And maybe the waxy feel of his skin. He was wearing his dark suit and red power tie. I got him under the arms and dragged him up the hill.

Deborah had tied a block and tackle to the top of the cannon, and she looped the rope around Tim's chest as soon as I put him down. She handed me the other end of the rope.

"You pull, I'll guide," she said.

I hoisted Tim up to the business end of the cannon. There was a moment of confusion as Deborah puzzled over the problem of actually getting him into the end of the gun. Finally, she shimmied up the barrel like a monkey and maneuvered him in head first. As she slid back down, the cannon leaned a little—maybe ten or twenty degrees from the perpendicular.

We observed a moment of silence looking at the cannon pointing out over the turkey farm. Tim's feet in their black wing tips stuck out of the end. It would be dark soon.

"I guess we're coming up on T-minus something," I said.

"Yes," Deborah said. She walked back to the bottom of the cannon.

"All systems go?" I asked.

She gave me a thumbs up.

Then she did something to the cannon and there was a tremendous wompf.

Tim flew from the end of the cannon and over the turkey pens.

"Uh oh," I said.

He'd been basically rolled into a ball when he left the end of the gun, but now his arms and legs unfurled, and he turned gracefully in the air just in time to splat face first into the big picture window of the farm house.

"Here comes Santa Claus," I said.

Deborah sprang into action. She grabbed my arm. "Come on!"

"Circle the wagons, Mildred," I babbled as she dragged me to the car. "The hippies are shooting dead people at us!"

So we were on the lam, I thought. Soon there would be road blocks, troops, police barricades. They'd be grabbing everyone within fifty miles of the turkey farm. They'd pen us up in camps until it was time for questioning—barbed wire and spotlights crossing and recrossing the dusty exercise yards. They'd line us up and some mean-looking cop with a bullhorn would shout, "Okay, who did it? Somebody better speak up."

He'd give us a moment to think it over. Then he'd turn loose the information-sniffing dogs, and there would be no way Deborah or I could hide the facts.

"Where are you going?" I shouted when I realized that she wasn't fleeing the scene but was instead driving past the turkey pens and into the farmer's front yard.

"Splashdown," she said. "We'll be in and out of there before they know what's happening. Get ready." She stood on the breaks, and the car swerved to a screaming stop. She was out of the car and running for the house before I could even get my door open.

I arrived just in time to hear her say, "Stand back! We've got to get him to a hospital!"

I stepped through the broken window. The Christmas tree had been hurled against the wall. Tim was still hugging it. Mrs. Manvil was on her knees holding on tight to the girl. You could see the family resemblance—wide eyes and slack, astonished mouths. Manvil himself stood over them, but I couldn't see his mouth under the big mustache.

I peeled Tim off the Christmas tree.

"We'll notify the authorities," Deborah said. "You folks just hang tight. What a thing to happen on Christmas Eve! Boy, the Lord sure does move in mysterious ways."

I thought she sounded a little hysterical, but maybe that was part of her plan. I dragged Tim through the window and across the yard to the car. Deborah backed out after me making stay-back and keep-calm motions with both hands at the Manvils.

I slammed the trunk on Tim and ran around and jumped in the shotgun seat. Deborah peeled out.

When we passed the Dairy Queen, she said, "Mission accomplished."

"Deborah, Deborah," I said, "do you really believe we just shot Tim into space?"

"Sadly, no," she said, "but we did do the next best thing."

"Meaning?"

"We shot him *at* space."

Her grin made my heart ache.

We stopped by her place to get Tim a change of clothes. Then we drove back to the funeral home.

"It's about time!" shouted the young guy who answered the bell. His attitude answered my question about how Deborah had gotten Tim out in the first place. Inside help.

"My God!" he said when he saw Tim. "What did you do to him?"

"Never mind," Deborah said. "Look, I brought new clothes."

We got Tim settled on his metal table.

She put a hand on the young man's arm. "I know you'll make him look good."

We left.

And Tim did look pretty good the next day at the funeral.

Deborah and I walked arm in arm past the casket.

"He looks a little squashed in the face," I whispered.

"It's the g-force," she said. "Look at him go!"

BEASTLY HEAT

The fact that the Dejorans looked a lot like humans hit Frank hard when he parted his living room curtains and turned his binoculars on the house across the street and saw the woman sitting on her screened porch, right out in the open where anyone who walked by could see her. He lowered the binoculars and knuckled his eyes in amazement.

Bees buzzed in the honeysuckle summer air, and Frank put another salty soda cracker covered with peanut butter and honey into his mouth, chewed thoughtfully, brushed crumbs from the front of his shirt, then put the binoculars back to his eyes and used the little ribbed roller to refine his focus.

If the woman had been human, she'd be a few years younger than Frank, maybe middle to late thirties. She wore a sleeveless white dress with big yellow flowers. Her brown hair looked damp as if she'd been misting herself to keep cool. She had a dreamy smile that gave her face a lazy summer look—just a pretty woman sitting on the porch some late July afternoon sipping lemonade and watching the world go by.

Frank wasn't fooled. It was the creature growing out of her shoulder that tipped him off. Joined twins. The big one looked like a woman. The little green one looked like nothing human. She offered her small companion a sip of lemonade. She seemed to be talking to it, sharing a secret.

He wished he could hear her voice, but she was a million miles away. More than a million. It all made sense suddenly. She was light-years away. The reason the woman could so openly show herself on her screened porch was that she was not on Earth at all. Somehow Frank had managed to defeat the void and peek across an interstellar distance to see this Dejoran woman talking to her second head. That had to be it. The universe was a place where even a self-educated scientist could figure things out, where solutions were possible, where nothing was unknowable, where logic ruled.

The Dejoran woman had nice eyes. He doubted she could see him across the galaxy without an instrument, but who knew about those alien eyes? The fact that she did see him hit home when she raised her right hand palm out like she was telling traffic to stop and then wiggled her fingers at him. She grinned across all that unimaginable distance, slapping him down and letting him fall in love as only a Terran with binoculars can, and being in love, he could see clearly that her little green head was looking at him, too, really looking, and he decided he loved her tiny twin as well. It was part of her charm. One of the million little things that made her who she was.

He had to get to her somehow.

Frank put his binoculars aside to do some serious noodling. Rocket ships were riddled with problems, not the least of which was he didn't have one. Could he project his mind across the void? He chuckled to himself. Astral projection was nonsense. On the other hand, he had recently been toying with the idea that Zeno's paradox of motion could be most elegantly resolved by postulating that the reason motion is impossible is that you are already everywhere. That is, if you are everywhere, the notion of motion is meaningless. So perhaps getting to the Dejoran woman was merely a matter of convincing himself that he was already there. Frank closed his eyes.

He pictured her porch. He imagined himself in front of her steps. He watched himself lift a foot and set it down on the first cracked wooden step. He felt himself rise as he pulled his weight up onto that foot. He opened his eyes. He was still sitting in his own living room.

Frank sighed. He picked up his binoculars and peered across at the love of his life, afraid suddenly that she would be gone. She was still there. But for how long? He jumped up and paced around the room looking for a travel plan.

Okay, how about geometry? As a person of scientific leanings, he would never be able to convince himself that he was already where he wanted to be. He needed to trick himself, and the best method for that was to apply more theory. Good. So the way to make two apparent places become one apparent place was to arrange the accouterments of the first place in such a way that it resonated with the second place; then the illusion of separateness would dissolve and the two places would seem to vibrate together. Geometry.

Frank spent some time pushing his furniture around the room, trying first one pattern then another. He rearranged the pictures on the walls. Nothing happened. Maybe he should roll up the rug?

Frank leaned against the wall to catch his breath. The necessary relationships among the objects at his place were obviously too subtle for him to stumble upon. He would have to resort to brute force. He would have to walk.

It would be a difficult journey. He would need protection against solar radiation. Frank opened his front hall closet and dug out his Greek fisherman's cap and put it on his head. He considered taking the binoculars, but the neck strap had broken years ago, and he decided he'd rather have both hands free to maneuver.

He checked all the windows. Who knew how long he'd be gone? He stepped out onto his porch, locked the front door, then jiggled the knob just to make sure. Once, twice, three times. Things could fool you.

He stood for a moment looking across the street. If he squinted his eyes a little he could actually see the wavering space/time warp. It appeared to be just to this side of the street. He couldn't tell how thick it was. Maybe he would simply be on her planet when he stepped through it. Not likely. There would probably be some distance of weirdness to traverse. Frank pulled the bill of his cap down a little and stepped off his porch and walked down the path to the street.

Up close he could see billions and billions of sparkling stars scattered across the hot pebbly surface of the road. Looking more closely, he saw the oily blackness of the street gave way to the purer, harder blackness of space. He lifted his right foot and held it suspended over the abyss, hesitant to make that first step, afraid that if he fell, he would fall forever.

Before putting his foot down, Frank glanced up to see the Dejoran woman watching him. She'd gotten to her feet, and now she beckoned to him, like a siren without a song. A drop of sweat ran down his side and he shivered.

Frank let his foot fall. He felt his body tingle as he passed through the hole in the universe. It was like walking on glass, like walking on an invisible roof over everything. Frank took another step then jumped back. Something he could clearly identify as the planet Saturn *and* as a station wagon rushed by him and screamed off into the void. More correctly, Frank thought, *he* had just screamed past Saturn.

He looked both ways for other planets, then hurried to the yellow line that marked the absolute boundary between the two worlds. He stopped for a moment to consider. Did he really want to do this? Could things ever be the same after this? Wouldn't this journey change him in some fundamental way? He looked back across the hell of space and time that he had just crossed. He thought of the Dejoran woman. He had to reach her. There was no turning back.

Frank came to her atmosphere and jumped out of the interstellar blackness and onto the sidewalk. He glanced up at the day star, and then, with dazzled eyes, looked at her pink grass. He stumbled up her walk and stood before her porch.

"Hello, Frank," she said as if she'd known him forever. "I've been hoping you'd come over. I'm Mabel."

"Afternoon, Mabel," he said, amazed that he could understand her, shocked that she had somehow intuited his name. Some kind of telepathy? He searched back in his memory. Had her lips matched her words? Yes, they had matched. So it was true. At some fundamental level everyone in the universe spoke English.

"I'm so glad we've finally met," she said. "Everyone says you're very nice."

Uh oh. People were talking about him. The fact that they were people on an entirely different planet was particularly troubling. He would have to keep his eyes peeled.

"Come on in and have a glass of lemonade, Frank."

"That sounds great." He climbed up on the porch and followed her into the house. Just inside, she took a sharp left turn down a short passage that opened up into a gleaming white and chrome kitchen. The smell of sweet basil drifted in the air.

Mabel opened the refrigerator and leaned in for the lemonade, giving Frank a chance to check out her bottom which he thought was very nice, but he felt the blood rush to his face when he saw the little green head looking at him from her shoulder.

"Ah, sorry," he said and looked away.

"What?" Mabel straightened up and turned to him with a pitcher of lemonade.

"Oh, never mind," he said.

Her grin got wider. "You were talking to Daisy, weren't you?"

Frank didn't know what to say. He'd never known how to act around people who named their body parts. This case was a little different, he admitted, but he was embarrassed nonetheless. He could see clearly that the differences between them were profound. He had reached across a galaxy to her, but could they ever really touch?

She came close and handed him a glass of lemonade. He could see small beads of sweat on her upper lip. Her smell made his head swim. His hand shook as he reached for the glass, and he shuddered, rattling the ice, when he touched her cool fingers.

At that moment he saw a fury of green wings from the corner of his eye, and he froze as a creature landed on his shoulder and dug talons into his flesh.

Confusion washed through him. He darted a glance at Mabel and saw that her green twin had not somehow gotten off her body. This was something new.

"Ah ha!" Mabel cried. "I knew you were our kind of people, Frank. Clancy likes you!" She waggled a finger in his direction. "Such a good boy!"

"So this is it," Frank said. He'd been taken over, occupied. Who would have thought? The woman had been bait. Dejorans were not born; they were made.

Frank felt himself merging with the creature on his shoulder, felt himself losing his will to resist, felt himself becoming Dejoran. He hoped the relationship would be symbiotic and not parasitic, but that was nothing he could control. He realized that he had never had control over anything, that he had never understood the universe, that there was nothing to do but reach out and touch someone. Huddle. Cuddle. Cling together. He put his hand out and Mabel took it.

Frank twisted around to look for the first time into the eyes of the creature that would ride him forever, his other half.

"Hello, big boy," said the little green head. "Wanna mambo?"

On the one hand, he was talking to himself, it was his little green head, so he should know very well the correct answer. On the other hand, there were subtleties to consider. Did his right hand know what his left hand was doing? Was escape still an option? And if it was still an option, did he really want to sacrifice the promise of fruity rum drinks, salsa, and flickering firelight as he danced the nights away with Mabel under these strange new stars? No. He didn't want to get away.

"Oh, yes," he said.

CEREMONY

There were still ten, maybe fifteen, kids lined up in front of the peppermint alcove when Santa died.

Brenda, as Santa's helper in her short red skirt, whose fake white fur hem just covered her red underwear, and a floppy red hat, whose white cotton puff ball hung over her left shoulder, was pretty sure that yelling "He's dead!" was not the way to bring x-mas cheer to the cranky kids and box and bag-burdened parents, all looking like they were waiting their turn for measles shots. Instead she stepped in front of the jolly old gentleman and urgently motioned Bob away from his camera.

Bob scanned her from head to toe, from toe to head as he approached, his fingers curling and uncurling in anticipation of touching her. "What is it?"

"I don't know how you're going to break it to them," Brenda whispered. "But your Santa just died."

"Died?" Bob darted a glance over her shoulder at Santa where he sat with his chin on his chest. "He can't do that! I just crossed the break even point."

A dad from the line called, "Hey! What's the hold up?"

Bob put on a smile and turned it on the waiting shoppers. "Nothing, nothing," he said. "We're almost ready."

"That'll be some trick," Brenda whispered.

"Now look." Bob grabbed her upper arm and leaned in close. "You get back there and work his head. Yeah, that's it. Get down on your knees behind his chair, and, you know, move his head around like he's talking. I'll lead the kids up, put them on his knee, and shoot them. Quick-like. We'll run them through so fast nobody'll notice."

"Work his head?"

Bob narrowed his eyes. "Don't give me static on this, Brenda. I make no money if I don't shoot these last ones. I can get another Santa tomorrow, and I can get another pretty pair of legs to replace you, too."

Brenda had been working for Bob for three days. Another day and she'd have the rent. Get fired now and she might spend the holidays on the Phoenix streets. At times like these, Brenda always heard Dolly Parton singing "Working 9 to 5" in her head.

"You do what you gotta do, kid," Dolly said.

"You're right." Brenda pictured Dolly as she would be tonight on her Christmas-at-Home special with her family in the Smokies. Brenda planned on cooking a turkey leg to eat while watching the show wrapped in the afghan she'd knitted herself for the occasion. She'd sing along.

Brenda walked behind Santa's chair and got down on one knee. Bob grinned and scurried away to the line, saying, "Who's next? Who's next?"

Brenda ran her right hand up under the white wig that was part of Santa's hat and grabbed a greasy handful of hair and pulled up his head. His scalp was still warm.

"Silver Bells," sang the Voice of the Mall. "Silver Bells."

Bob led a wide-eyed little girl away from the line where her mother stood wrestling with her packages and scowling. Bob took the girl under the arms, sat her on Santa's lap, and hurried back to his camera. The girl looked up at Santa, then she looked at Brenda peering over Santa's left shoulder.

"Santa wants to know your name," Brenda said.

"Crystal."

"That's a nice name," Brenda said. "Like the singer."

"What is this?" Crystal's mom called from the line. "I want to hear some ho ho hos!"

Bob jerked up his chin at Brenda and lasergunned her with his eyes.

Brenda turned her face down so they couldn't see her mouth and in a voice as deep as she could make it said, "Ho ho ho." She jerked Santa's head up and down and wagged it from side to side, hoping for a bowlful of jelly effect.

Crystal wrinkled his nose. "I think Santa pooped his pants."

"I know. I know." Brenda whispered. "Isn't he silly?" She turned Santa's face so he would appear to be whispering in her ear. "Santa wants to know what you want for Christmas, Crystal. Don't you, Santa?" She nodded his head.

Crystal straightened her shoulders and rattled off a long list of merchandise.

"Okay," Bob said. "Okay. I got it." He rushed up and plucked the girl from Santa's lap and set her on her feet.

"I didn't get to finish my list!" Crystal yelled as her mother dragged her into the river of mall people.

"You don't have to do this, Brenda," Dolly whispered in her ear.

Brenda's fingers were stiff, and a dull ache spread through her hand and up her arm. The weight of Santa's head was like holding up a bowling ball. She just wanted to let go. She just wanted to go home.

"But what about the rent, Dolly?"

"Something will turn up," Dolly said. "It always does."

"It always does," Brenda said. "I don't have to do this."

Santa's head twisted suddenly in her hand. His skull turned to ice, freezing her fingers in place. He opened his mouth, and his breath was spoiled milk in her face. "Deliver unto me that which is mine, Brenda," he said.

Brenda yelped and tore her hand from his head and jumped up. Santa slumped forward until his head hung between his knees.

"Hey!" Bob rushed up and knelt down in front of Santa and pushed him back up. "What the hell are you doing?" His voice was a mean hiss.

"We don't have to do this," Brenda said. She could see the remaining parents huddled in hushed conference, the children hugging their legs and hanging onto their hands and staring with wide eyes at Santa slouched in his big chair.

"You'd better hope you didn't screw this up, Brenda." Bob hurried over to the parents and joined the huddle.

A moment later, a man prodded a small boy forward. "Take him next," the man said.

Bob pulled the boy to Santa. "Get back in your place, Brenda."

"But surely they know now!"

Bob glanced back at the parents. "Turns out they don't care," he said. "They just want to get this done."

The boy's father smiled at Brenda and made the okay sign with his finger and thumb.

The rent. Her turkey leg. And Dolly's show tonight. Bob wouldn't pay her if she left now. Brenda looked out into the faces of the Mall People. They stood behind the red rope at the edge of the peppermint candy cane alcove and worshiped her, their faces glowing. A man lifted his shopping bag and rattled it at her. A woman did the same. Then they were all doing it. Their voices rose, pleading, insisting.

"Bring back the sun, Brenda."

"Make the corn grow, Brenda."

"Seed the New Year sales, Brenda!"

Her head swam with their voices. Brenda wanted to hide, wanted them to take their eyes off her, but the Mall People would have their way. She stepped behind Santa and crouched down again. Bob put the boy on Santa's knee.

When she raised Santa's head, the boy took one look at Santa's eyes and screamed. Bob snapped the photo and plucked the child from Santa's lap. Brenda turned Santa's head this way and that, as if he were peering around for the nastiness that could make a child scream so.

Bob and the boy's father stood looking at the Polaroid as it developed. Bob nudged the man in the ribs with his elbow. "Hang onto this picture," he said. "It'll be fantastic ammunition when the kid's a teenager. Next! Next!"

Brenda turned Santa's head around so she could look into his rolled white eyes. His mouth had twisted into a nasty grin under his cotton moustache.

"No," Brenda said. "Just no." She dropped his head and stood up.

"Hey wait!" Bob snatched at her as she pushed past him. "We aren't finished!"

"What are you?" a woman hugging a weeping toddler to her chest said. "Some kind of Scrooge?"

"I'll be home for Christmas," Brenda said.

She ran from the peppermint alcove, scattering the Mall People from her path. The Voice of The Mall moaned in despair, and shops darkened as she passed them.

POOP

Sometimes they felt like kids again, his arm around her shoulders, her arm around his waist, standing over the sleeping baby, this late-in-life lazy sperm, test tube wonder they'd named Lewis, because Lewis was a popular name these days (and you can call him Lewie), and just because Lewie's parents were in their forties didn't mean he had to walk around with an out-of-fashion name. Hey, years ago, they might have named him after one of Marilyn's favorite causes. So, what's your name, little boy? And he'd look down at his shoes and mutter, Save-The-Whales, sir.

You couldn't expect the sailing to always be smooth. "It's not like getting another cat," he said or she said and they agreed that no, it was not like getting another cat. Even the cats they already had knew it was not like getting another cat. Not so much the smell of talcum and sour diapers, nor the fact that the guest room now had a permanent resident. It was more a wound-tight constant watchfulness. Karl and Marilyn knew babies weren't made out of glass, but knowing that didn't mean they weren't on constant alert for danger. The cats all had the same new name, and that new name was "get away from there!"

One evening when Karl went into his Honey-I'm-home routine, she rushed out of the shadows sobbing with a bundle and pushed it into his arms and ran out of the room.

Well, it was his turn. He put little Lewis down on the couch and pulled at the Velcro tabs and peeled back the diaper and took a look at the load Lewis had left. It seemed to consist entirely of perfectly formed discrete bits, brown and soft looking, and shaped like an assortment of threaded nuts and bolts. Aside from the usual bad smells Karl had come to expect, there was also a hint of machine oil. Jeeze, what had the kid been eating?

"Hey, Marilyn!" he said. "Come on back out here. You gotta see this."

"No," she called. "That's just the point. When it's your turn, I definitely don't have to see it."

He grabbed Lewie's feet, pulled the dirty diaper away and made a neat package of it. He hoisted the baby up higher and washed his bottom.

From somewhere far away, Karl could hear music, like the local philharmonic had decided to take a few turns around the block. He looked back over his shoulder at the window. The sound didn't seem to be coming from the street. In fact, it seemed to be coming from Lewis. Feed your baby little radios and he will forever have a song in his heart? Karl moved to put his ear down on the baby's stomach, but first strategically positioned his hand—having already been hosed in the traditional first defiant act of the son lashing out at the father—and listened. Yes, there it was—tummy music.

"Hey, Marilyn, the kid's playing Bach!" Karl called.

"Concerto? Or symphony?" she asked.

"You could come listen for yourself."

"Not a chance," she said.

The music stopped suddenly. Maybe it had been coming from the apartment below. Karl fixed Lewis up with a fresh diaper.

Lewis got a look on his face like he'd eaten a bowling ball and maybe now was the time to throw a strike.

"Oh no," Karl said. "Not again. Not so soon."

The diaper bulged around the baby's thighs. It bunched and unbunched like a fist in a glove.

When all movement finally stopped, Karl peeled the diaper down. Small brown birds burst into the air and flew away in all directions.

Karl jerked away with a startled cry.

"You can knock off the sound effects," Marilyn called. "I'm not going to look."

The birds settled on the curtain rod above the big picture window. They spent a few moments squabbling and preening and elbowing for position before settling in to stony silence and sidelong glances.

"This is serious, Marilyn," he said, and she must have heard something serious in his voice because a moment later she appeared at the kitchen door.

"What in the world?" she said when she spotted the birds.

"Lewis," Karl said.

He looked back down at Lewis, and Lewis pumped his legs and waved his arms. His diaper was not too messy. In fact, Karl couldn't tell if what was there had been left by Lewis or by the birds. Marilyn sat down on the couch and Lewis stretched his arms back over his head and rolled up his eyes to look at her. She absently tickled his nose and he giggled and snatched at her hand. Running mostly on automatic now, Karl washed the baby again and changed his diaper.

He looked at Marilyn over the baby and she looked at him.

"Where did the birds come from, Karl?" she asked.

"From Lewis," he said. "They were in his diaper."

"Don't be silly," she said. "Really. There must be a window open somewhere."

"Sure," he said, "that must be it."

But he didn't believe it, and she could see he didn't believe it, and he could see that she didn't believe it either. Lewis gurgled and giggled and his parents, long practiced in marital telepathy, zapped thoughts back and forth above his head. We can handle this. We're adults. We can do it. No we can't. We're children ourselves. What do we know about babies? No one told us anything about this. What are we going to do? I wish my mother was here. I wish your mother was here, too, or my mother. Your mother wouldn't know what to do. What's wrong with my mother? Would you shut up about your mother?

Lewis rumbled and filled his pants again.

"I'm afraid to look," Karl said.

Marilyn reached over the baby and pulled the Velcro tabs.

A multitude of mice exploded from Lewie's diaper. Karl and Marilyn leaped up off the couch, yelling. The mice scrambled over the baby's stomach and legs and across the couch and off onto the floor, definitely hitting the ground running, and the birds screamed and leaped into flight, crossing and recrossing in the air, never quite colliding, swooping down on the fleeing mice, not catching any as the mice hot-footed it under the furniture. The cats, no longer cowering, dashed around after the mice and jumped and swatted at the birds.

Marilyn covered the baby with her body. Karl stood over them both, waving away the birds and kicking at the mice the cats had flushed from under the furniture.

"We might as well be on the moon," Karl said. There was absolutely no one to ask. So many friends, but none of their friends would have a clue about this.

"What?"

Check the baby books. They had an entire shelf of baby books.

They had had lots of time for research. They hadn't gone into this with their eyes closed. Or maybe call the pediatrician. Doctor, is it normal for my baby to be pooping birds and mice?

"We need someone to tell us what to do." Karl said.

"Shouldn't we know what to do?" Marilyn asked.

"Yes," Karl said. "We should know what to do." But even as he said it he could see that they both realized they would never know what to do. There would never be a single time they would be able to say for sure, yes, this is the right thing to do—this definitely is right for you, Lewis. This is what should happen or this is how it should be. We're absolutely right to say you can't go there. We know what we're talking about when we say you should do this instead of that. Father knows best. Listen to your mother.

There came wet sputtering flatulence from Lewis, gastrointestinal distress, but also words, surely words, muttering, whispering, a gravelly voice from a place no words had ever come before. It was as if the speaker were trying all of the languages on Earth, looking for the one that would work in this situation. Then there was a tremendous clearing of the throat, so to speak.

The birds retreated to the curtain rod again, taking their seats like theater patrons after an intermission. Karl and Marilyn sat down again on either side of Lewis and waited to see what he would produce next.

What Lewis produced next was unearthly and smelly, obviously from elsewhere, and it seemed to surprise the baby as much as his parents. Someone said, "Hello, Father. Hello, Mother."

Karl looked at Marilyn. "Er . . . hello," he said.

"But who is speaking?" she whispered.

Karl didn't know. He shook his head. "Maybe a ghost?"

"You're suggesting my baby's butt is haunted?"

"Do you suppose we could think of these as his first words?" Karl asked.

"Will you two shut up and listen for a moment?"

"You shouldn't tell your elders to shut up," Karl said.

"I have come back to speak of a time some fifteen years in the future, when you will be faced with what might seem like a trivial decision to you."

Karl reached over the baby and put his hands on Marilyn's shoulders. They leaned together, head to head, looking down at Lewis.

After a silence in which Karl suddenly worried that maybe they'd simply gone crazy, and didn't know whether that was a comfort or not, the voice spoke again. "There will come the time when Lewis wants to attend a camp out in the desert in which the other guests will be both girls and boys."

"Yes?" Marilyn said.

"You'll worry about beer and drugs that haven't even been invented yet."

"Oh, no," Marilyn said.

"You'll worry about sex and diseases that haven't even been invented yet."

"And?" Karl asked. He suddenly knew that he should pay particular attention to that look on Lewie's face. It would be a look he would need to watch out for in the future.

"You must let him go," the voice said.

WHITE GUYS IN SPACE

1.

A fter an obligatory period of lies and damn lies, the 104th congress repealed the 1960s, and Worldmaster Jones, secret CEO for AmerEarth Corp, and his right-hand hatchet man, Coordinator Grey, popped into existence.

"Boy, it's about time," Jones said.

"You got that right, Worldmaster," said Grey.

Jones rang for his secretary.

"Yes, Worldmaster?"

"Have the boys get my helicar ready, Nancy," Jones said, "and bring in a couple of cups of coffee."

2.

Not to mention the bug-eyed lobster men from Alpha Centauri.

RAY VUKCEVICH

3.

"Wow! Would you look at all the knobs!" Joe said when he peeked into the control cabin of the spaceship. Joe, who was doing simultaneous degrees in atomic physics, medieval studies, entomology, philosophy, hotel/motel management, linguistics, and electrical engineering at Yale, knew a thing or two about spaceships.

His buddy Frank, home for the holidays from Harvard where he was majoring in chemistry, mathematics, Victorian detective fiction, farm management, and computer science, rubbed a hand across his blond crewcut and joined Joe at the window of the unfinished craft. "Gosh," he said, "do you think it'll really work?"

"You've got to have faith in our friend the atom, boys." Doc pulled his head out of the access hatch and waved a socket wrench at Frank. "Of course it'll work!"

Doc, who had always been just a little too far out for the universities, had streaks of gray running through his unruly hair, and a perpetually preoccupied look on his craggy face. Joe guessed he was in his forties. He wore a white lab coat and black loafers.

"Hey, what are you guys doing?" someone called from the garage doorway.

"Uh oh," Doc said. "Trouble."

Frank elbowed Joe in the ribs. "You can close your mouth now," he said. "It's just Nancy."

"Hi, Doctor Tim!" The young woman stepped into the garage and smiled, and Joe's heart missed a beat.

4.

Meanwhile the slimy lobster men from Alpha Centauri, who had been going somewhere else entirely before the sixties had been

222

repealed, turned their scaly attention to Earth, and what they saw they liked. By the time Joe and Frank helped Doc get the spaceship upright and onto its tail fins and aimed at the moon, the lobster men only had bug-eyes for Earth women.

5.

"You can't go," Frank said.

"I can, too!"

"Tell her she can't go, Doc," Frank said.

"You can't go, Nancy."

"Hey, why not?" Joe spoke up suddenly, and the two other men looked at him like he'd gone crazy.

"Look, you guys," Nancy said, "this is the story of the century. You've got to let me go along. The first people on the moon! I was born to cover this story."

"That's the first *men*," Frank said. "The first men on the moon."

"Is that why you're taking Spot?"

"Hey! Spot's a spacedog."

6.

Actually, this could be to our advantage," Worldmaster Jones said. "Let's see if we can't cut a deal with the seafood."

"But what could we have that they'd want?" asked Coordinator Grey.

7.

"Ten," Doc said.

"What?"

"He said 'ten.'"

"Ten what?"

"Nine," Doc said.

"I thought you said he said 'ten?'"

"Eight," Doc said.

"I give up." Joe threw up his hands and leaned back in his contoured spacechair and looked up at the sky through the forward viewports. It would be a long time before he saw that sky again. He wondered if he might lose Nancy altogether. Could their relationship hold up under the strain of his just going off into space, right after they'd first met? Well, a man has to do what a man has to do. He would suffer this sweet anguish in stony silence.

"Seven," Doc said.

"Maybe you'd better start flipping switches," Frank said. He made a few quick calculations with his slipstick and jotted down the results on a pad on the arm of his spacechair.

"Six," Doc said.

"Good idea," Joe said. "Doc seems to be preoccupied. As you know, Frank, he's done all the calculations for the trip in his head."

"Five," Doc said.

"Just checking," Frank grumbled. He put his slipstick away. "Did you remember to close the supply hatch?"

"Four," Doc said.

"Me?" Joe finished flipping a bank of switches before turning to look at Frank. "You were supposed to close that hatch. Hey, Doc, I think Frank forgot to close the supply hatch."

"Three," Doc said.

"Look," Frank said, "I clearly remember asking you to close the hatch."

"Two," Doc said.

"Darn it, Frank," Joe said. He unsnapped his harness and swung his legs around off his chair.

"One," Doc said.

"Oh, sit still," Frank said. He unsnapped his own harness. "If you're going to pout, I'll go shut it."

"Blast off!" Doc cried.

8.

"Something has risen from the surface of the planet," Z'p said, and then dropped flat to the floor in a show of respect.

"So, shoot it down," Hivekeeper B'b said. "Do I have to think of everything?"

"Thinking of everything is your job," muttered Z'p.

"What did you say?"

"I said we're too far out to shoot it down, Hivekeeper."

"How long before we get to the moon?"

"We're almost there now."

9.

The blue and white curve of Earth had been visible briefly before Doc aimed the nose of the ship at the moon. Now there was nothing much to see and nothing much to do but eat lunch. Joe, Frank, Doc, and Spot floated around the control cabin eating pork'n'beans from cans and drinking orange pop.

"What was that noise?" Frank asked.

"Noise?" Doc said.

"I didn't hear anything," Joe said.

"Arf," said Spot.

"Well, I heard it," Frank said. He left his spoon sticking in his can of pork'n'beans and the can floating in the air and swam down to the door to the supply closet. He seized the handle and threw open the door. Nancy tumbled out with a yelp.

10.

Meanwhile, back on Earth, Mrs. Jones put a perfect pot roast on the dining room table. She arranged the carving knife and fork on the platter and adjusted the angles of their handles so they would be just where the Worldmaster expected them to be when he reached for them to carve the roast. She hurried back into the kitchen for the mashed potatoes. The doorbell rang.

"Oh, double darn!" she said. She glanced around quickly to see if anyone had heard her. Worldmaster Jones would not tolerate rough language. He would be in his den smoking his pipe. Would he answer the door on his own? Well, maybe when . . . maybe when . . . well, maybe when heck got a lot colder. Oh my, such thoughts. The doorbell rang again.

"Oh, Worldmaster Jones," she called, "would you mind getting that, dear?"

Of course, he would get the door, the old bear, but he wouldn't like it. "Where's Billy?" he growled as he came out of his den.

"Here I am, Worldmaster," Billy said coming down the stairs in his baseball outfit. He snatched the cap off his head when he saw the fire smoldering in his father's eyes.

"And do you suppose you could get the door?" Worldmaster Jones rattled his newspaper at the boy.

"I thought Mom would get it," Billy said on his way to the front door.

Worldmaster Jones paused in the doorway of his den so he could see who was at the door. His wife did the same from her spot by the dining room table. Billy opened the door.

A young man in a neat black suit and a thin tie greeted Billy. "Hello, is your mother or father home?"

"Well." Billy glanced back at Worldmaster Jones, who pretended to read his paper.

The young man must have figured it out. He stepped up the volume of his voice. "I'm asking for donations for basic services." He had a tin can with a thin slit for change cut into the top. "Police, fire, city services, roads and streets, health care and food for the poor, schools from kindergarten to the university. You know, everything but the military. Can I count on you folks?"

"Dinner's ready," Mrs. Jones called brightly.

Worldmaster Jones stepped forward. "Thank you, young man, but we gave at the office." He closed the door.

11.

"If I hadn't pulled that hatch closed behind me, you'd all be sucking vacuum!" Nancy said. "It's not like you can just put me out." When she wasn't talking, she was chewing her gum a mile a minute, and Joe wondered what it would be like to shut her up with a kiss. "I mean you really wouldn't do that, would you, Doctor Tim?"

"I don't know," Frank said. "What do you think, Doc?"

"Of course we won't put her out!" Joe pushed off the wall and did a superman dive for her, but she grabbed a handhold and moved out of the way before he arrived. Joe sailed on past her with a goofy smile on his face and crashed head first into the wall.

"Besides," he said rubbing his head, "we could use a woman's touch around here. Aren't you guys getting tired of pork'n'beans?"

Frank admitted grudgingly that he for one was getting tired of pork'n'beans.

"Arf!" said Spot.

"And I can finally get a cup of coffee," Doc said.

12.

The lobster men from Alpha Centauri landed on the back side of the moon and scuttled from the sunshine into deep lunar caverns and tunnels they dug as they went along. Soon the moon was infested with lobsters.

"So, what do we do now?" Z'p asked.

"We wait for the women," Hivekeeper B'b said.

13.

Joe's hand might have been a creature with a mind of its own as it skulked like a white spider across the back of the spacechair behind Nancy's head. A few more inches and he could drop his arm around her shoulders.

The moon was huge and bright in the forward viewports.

"Oh, look how big it is," Nancy said.

"What?" Joe felt his face go red.

Frank chuckled wickedly.

"Arf," said Spot.

"Get ready to land on the moon, boys," Doc said.

14.

"What I don't understand, Worldmaster Jones," Coordinator Grey said, "is how your secretary got onto a spaceship heading for the moon."

"If you can't spot a spy when you see one, Coordinator Grey," Worldmaster Jones said, "I begin to doubt your abilities."

15.

Joe, Frank, Doc, and Spot pressed their faces against the glass as they gazed out at the lunar landscape. Nancy jumped and poked and pushed and pinched from behind, trying to squeeze in for a look herself. They'd gotten into the form-fitting spacesuits Doc had designed, and each carried a fishbowl helmet. In fact, Doc carried two, Spot being unable to carry his own.

"Ow," Frank said when Nancy pinched his ear. He moved away from the viewport and she took his place. "Say, Doc," he said, "how come you just happened to have a babe suit on hand for Nancy?"

"You think that 'be prepared' stuff is just words?" Doc asked.

"Oh, look," Nancy said.

"What can they be?" Joe asked.

"Moon monsters?" Nancy offered.

"What are you talking about?" Frank asked.

"I don't think so," Doc said. "They seem to be wearing life-support systems themselves. If they were native to the moon they wouldn't need spacesuits."

"Well, I think we should go out and meet them," Nancy said. "I could get an interview."

"So, you're feeling like a snack?" Joe asked.

"Girls." Frank rolled his eyes.

"Look," Nancy said, "they're waving at us."

16.

"What are you doing, Hivekeeper?" Z'p was mystified at the strange antics of his leader. The Hivekeeper bounced up and down on his back legs and clicked both of his claws above his head.

"It's the Intergalactic Babe Call," the Hivekeeper said. "If there are women in there, they won't be able to resist this."

17.

"Me first," Nancy said, elbowing her way up to the airlock.

"No way!" Frank cried. "If anyone should be the first man on the moon, it should be Doc."

"Well, even if I go first," Nancy said, "Doctor Tim can still be the first man on the moon."

"She does have a point." Joe pulled Frank aside.

"What point?"

"Well, a point of politeness," Joe said. "It's always Ladies First."

"Well, I don't know."

"In your heart you know I'm right, Frank."

"See? That's the trouble of having women on board in the first place," Frank said. "I knew we'd come to a conundrum like this sooner or later."

Air whooshed out of the cabin.

"Hey!" Frank shouted. "She didn't do the doors right!"

"Close it!" Joe shouted. "Watch out!" He grabbed Spot by the tail before the spacedog could be blown out onto the lunar surface.

Frank got the airlock door closed. They hurried to the viewport to see what had happened to Nancy.

Nancy, the glass bubble of her helmet reflecting billions and billions of stars, put out her hands in a peaceful gesture and walked toward the line of lobster men.

"Oh, Nancy," Joe whispered.

When Nancy got to the line of lobster men, they grabbed her and scrambled off like a swarm of cockroaches.

"Come on!" Joe shouted. "We've got to get out there and save her."

18.

The lobster men dragged Nancy deep into the bowels of the moon.

"So, what did you think of Earth when you first saw it?" Nancy was trying to do her job. "Tell me, do you guys have plans for an invasion of the planet itself? What do you do when you're not waging interstellar wars? Are there any more like you at home?"

The lobster men tossed Nancy into a rock chamber and closed the door behind her. Sitting at a table in the middle of the room were the biggest lobster man yet, and a human being.

"Worldmaster Jones!" Nancy exclaimed.

"Yes, it's me," Jones said. "Did you think for a moment that you fooled me by pretending to be my secretary back on Earth? Don't make me laugh. The moment you walked in, Nancy, I knew you were a perky, gum-snapping, wisecracking girl reporter."

"So, where do we go from here?" Nancy asked. "I mean just what are you up to? Selling out the human race to these lobster guys? And what happens to me?"

"As for your first question," Worldmaster Jones said, "you shouldn't worry your pretty little head over such matters. As for your second question, you can make yourself useful. I've been dying to show B'b here what a good cup of coffee is like. You'll find the proper equipment through that tunnel."

19.

Frank touched helmets with Joe. "It's hopeless," he said. "There are just too many tunnels. We'll never find her."

"We'll keep looking," Joe said.

"Arf," Spot said.

"Hey! Did you hear that?"

"Hear what?"

"Spot," Joe said. "I heard Spot. There must be air in here!"

"Arf," Spot said again, confirming Joe's speculation.

"So who's going to take his helmet off first?" Frank asked.

"We could draw straws."

"Where's Doc?" Frank asked. "He ought to be here to take his chances with the rest of us."

"Oh, fiddlesticks. Are we going to have to rescue him. too?"

"We could just pull Spot's helmet off," Frank said.

"Arf!" said Spot.

"You really are a rascal aren't you, Frank."

"It was a joke." Frank reached down to Spot, but the spacedog backed away, a little snarl curling his lip.

"Oh well," Joe said. "Here goes." He pulled his helmet off and took a deep breath.

Doc came around the corner carrying his helmet under his arm and dragging a sack through the moon dust.

"What you got there, Doc?"

"Bag o' swords, boys," he said. "This ought to even out the odds."

"Yeah!"

"Man oh man!"

The guys spent a few minutes slicing the air with sabers, and then Doc called them back to order. "This way, boys," he said.

20.

"So." Worldmaster Jones put his cup of coffee down and looked deep into the many-faceted eyes of the Hivekeeper. "Do we have a deal?"

"Let me get this straight," Hivekeeper B'b said, "you get the secret of faster-than-light travel, and we get a very large number of Earth

women. You wouldn't be trying to bamboozle the old Hivekeeper
would you, Worldmaster?"

"Whatever do you mean, B'b?"

"He means," Nancy said, "I'm the only woman on the moon, and
one is not exactly a very large number." She reached around the
Worldmaster and filled his cup.

"Maybe I didn't make myself clear," Worldmaster Jones said. "At
this very moment, Coordinator Grey is rounding up boatloads of the
most, er . . . well, spirited of our coffee makers, toothsome downtown
honeys gleaned from the streets of our major cities, shapely dames
from our secretarial pools, beach chicks and housewives—you name it.
By the time you whisper in my ear the secret of your faster-than-light
drive, the moon will be swarming with women!"

21.

Back to back with Frank, Joe fought his way through a phalanx of clicking and clacking, snapping and biting lobsters. Suddenly, way down
the tunnel, he saw Spot run out and bark at him and then run around
the bend in the tunnel and a moment later he was back barking again.

"Let's work our way down that way," Joe huffed at Frank. The two
men chopped their way through the lobster men toward the spacedog.
They broke free of the melee and ran. Joe scooped up Spot as they
passed into the tunnel. A light gleamed at the far end, and the lobsters
seemed reluctant to follow them.

They rushed into a chamber where they saw an Earth man drinking
coffee with a huge lobster. Nancy hovered around the table with a silver
coffee pot.

"Joe!" she cried.

Joe took three giant steps across the floor and lopped off the head
of the huge lobster.

"Oh yuck," Nancy said, knowing without asking who would be expected to clean up the blue blood splattered everywhere.

"Hold it right there," Worldmaster Jones said. He produced a spacepistol, like magic, and shot Frank in the shoulder.

"Hey, no fair!" Joe cried. "You said to hold it and we held it. What's with the shooting?"

"I just wanted you to know I was serious," Worldmaster Jones said.

Spot waddled over to Frank where he lay on the floor holding his shoulder. The spacedog whined and licked Frank's face. "So you're my friend in the end, after all," Frank said.

"You'll never get away with this," Joe told Worldmaster Jones.

"You idiot," the Worldmaster said. "You don't even know what I'm trying to get away with. I could tell you before I kill you, but since you're the only one who doesn't know what I'm up to, I don't think I'll bother. Say your prayers and die puzzled."

"Nancy?" Joe reached out to her with his eyes. "If a miracle happens, and we somehow get out of this, will you marry me?"

"Oh, Joe," she said, eyes suddenly moist, face all aglow and out of focus.

Before Worldmaster Jones could shoot Joe down like a dog, Doc rushed into the room with a machine. He put the device on the floor and dropped to his knees in front of it.

Joe used the diversion to slip over to Nancy and put his arm around her shoulders.

Doc's machine hummed and buzzed. Worldmaster Jones leaped to his feet. Spot tugged at Frank until Frank rolled over and crawled to Joe and Nancy.

"What is it, Doc?" Joe asked.

"The missing sixties," Doc said.

"Until this very moment," Joe said, "I'd forgotten they were missing."

"Shut up, Joe," Doc said, twisting knobs like crazy. "We're tuning in."

"But we don't understand, Doctor Tim."

"Please be quiet, Nancy," Doc said. "We're turning on."

"Arf?" Spot said.

"That's right, Spot," Doctor Tim said and got to his feet and stretched out his hands to his young friends. "We're dropping out."

They linked hands and made a circle around Doc's machine, and the machine reached through the clouds of cold corporate atomotraps and gotmines regularly tossed like sand into the eyes of the world and spread the curtains of patriotic songs they hadn't until that moment realized were masking the sounds of pain and protest and waved away the smoke from huddling masses of the formerly invisible homeless and hungry and seized the missing years and pulled them singing and swaying back into existence and the air filled with springtime, and flowers fell like warm rain, and the sun came down into the bowels of the moon, just so it could set again in glorious shades of purple and green.

"Noooooooo!" Worldmaster Jones cried as he went out of phase with everything and faded away.

The lobster men packed up their things and went home.

"So, Nancy," Joe said. "Now that we're safe, how about marrying me?"

She slipped a hand into the back pocket of his jeans and squeezed. "Let's sleep on it," she said.

WHISPER

And then she fired her parting shot. "And not only *that*," she said, as if "*that*" hadn't been quite enough, "you snore horribly!" "I do not," I said. "I definitely do not snore." I was talking to her back. "You're making it up!" I was talking to the door. "Someone else would have mentioned it!" I was talking to myself.

Mistakes were made, relationships fell apart, and hurtful things were said. Life was like that.

In the days that followed, I rearranged all the furniture. I threw out everything in the refrigerator. I bought new spices—savory, anise, cumin, cracked black pepper—and packaged macaroni and cheese and powdered soups. Anchovies. Things Joanna didn't like. I left the toilet seat up all the time and dropped my clothes wherever I took them off. I got a new haircut and collected brochures for a getaway to Panama. I looked at a red convertible but didn't buy it.

Her crack about me snoring wouldn't leave me alone, probably because it poked something that had always worried me. My father had snored. I remembered listening to him snore all the way down the hall and around the corner. I always thought it must be awful to be in there with him. Maybe it ran in the family, like baldness or alcoholism.

The solution, once it hit me, seemed obvious. I would record myself sleeping. I had nothing that would record such a long time, so I went to an audio store and bought an expensive machine that would do the job. I used some of the money I'd saved by not buying the red convertible.

I set it up on the dresser across the room at the foot of the bed. I poured myself a nightcap, drank it during the eleven o'clock news, brushed my teeth, turned on the recorder, got into bed and squirmed around restlessly for over an hour, listening to the possibly imaginary whir and hiss of magnetic tape moving through the mechanism.

The next day, there was no time to check the tape as I hurried through my morning ritual and left for work. I was tempted, but I couldn't afford to be late. Then I got busy and didn't think about it again until bedtime the next night.

I made myself a complicated drink and a plate of crackers with anchovies and cheese and sat down on the foot of my bed. I don't know exactly what I expected. I was a little apprehensive. I stretched up and switched on the machine.

There were the sounds of me changing positions and sighing as I tried to get to sleep. I listened and ate a few crackers then stood up and held down the fast-forward button.

There were long periods of silence. No snoring. The house was quiet, too, with that late night stillness that isn't really so quiet when you finally listen, and the two silences got mixed together until I was listening hard and eating crackers and not caring about the crumbs in my bed.

I continued sampling a moment here and there and then moving on. "Ah ha," I said. "I knew it."

There was a long embarrassing fart an hour or so into the night, but absolutely no snoring. I heard something move in the kitchen like stuff settling in the plastic trash bag, a totally familiar sound. In fact, I couldn't tell if it was on the tape or had just happened in real time. I heard the house creaking and the distant sounds of traffic and once an auto horn. Several hours later, a siren screamed in the distance, and my sleeping self moaned. The 3:00 A.M. train went by, five miles to the south. I had stopped hearing that whistle a long time ago. It was comforting somehow to hear it again. I speeded the tape forward.

I was home free.

Joanna had been jerking me around.

But then a woman said, "Shush!' and giggled softly, and I gasped and jerked my hand up and drenched the front of my shirt with my drink.

I looked around wildly, thinking it was Joanna talking, thinking maybe it hadn't been on the tape, thinking maybe she was standing right behind me, but most of me knew she wasn't there. And the superspeed scenario I played in my mind where she'd sneaked into my bedroom last night to talk on my tape was stupid. Besides it hadn't even been her voice.

"Just look at him," the voice whispered.

I could hear someone moving around in the room. The rustle of clothing, the bump of a leg maybe hitting the side of the dresser or the chair by the window.

"Sure," a man whispered, "he's adorable."

The woman giggled again.

Then nothing.

I carefully put my glass down on the floor. I felt cold. My ears were ringing and my breathing was fast and shallow. I pulled off my wet shirt and threw it at the bathroom door.

The tape still moved but was silent.

I sat there listening for maybe an hour. Then I told myself I had imagined the whole thing. I got up and rewound the tape and played it again.

"Just look at him," the woman whispered.

I spent the rest of the night listening to every inch of the tape. You would think listening to over eight hours of tape would take more than eight hours, but I made good use of the fast-forward button, and by morning, I was pretty sure that little snatch of conversation was all there was.

I considered calling in sick, but then I would probably fall asleep, and I wasn't ready to fall asleep yet. I showered and shaved and got dressed.

Things were too bright outside. The feeling was like an old memory of all-nighters in college and crawling out into the daylight finally and feeling like everything must surely be an elaborate set in a movie about someone else. I remembered the way Abby, my first true love, looked in those days, warm young woman, zoomed in tight, big distorted nose, morning close up, sleepy head, kiss kiss, an echoing dress-store dummy somehow moving, smiling too big, too many teeth. Good morning, Sunshine. And later, the coffee so deeply black and hot against my own teeth. Eggs over easy so you can paint bright yellow daffodils with your toast. Thick slabs of bacon.

"You're doing the Zen breakfast thing, aren't you?" Abby bumped me with her shoulder. We sat side by side at the counter because the place was always too full to get a booth in the morning.

Where had she gone? I remembered dreaming over and over again that I had accidentally killed her and hidden her body in a closet or out in the barn or under the bed, and for years and years and years I was forced to take care of it so no one would ever find out. I finished school and got good work, met a woman named Louisa, married her, fathered children, lost them but got weekends, met Joanna, all the time playing a complicated juggling game involving plastic bags and big trunks to keep Abby's body hidden.

I suddenly wondered if that was Abby on the tape.

"More coffee?"

"What?" I snapped out of it long enough to nod and smile at the woman with the coffee pot. "Yes, please."

I looked around. This was not the diner from my past. This was the restaurant down the block from my office. I never stopped in here for breakfast, but judging by the remains on my plate, I had stopped in for breakfast today. I glanced at my watch. I was late. I finished my coffee too quickly, burned my mouth, left a tip, paid the bill, and hurried off.

Out in the bright morning crowd of busy people all moving so deliberately toward important tasks, I knew very well I hadn't killed Abby and kept her body hidden all these years. That was just something I had dreamed more than once. But I was drawing a blank on just what had happened to her. I couldn't really bring her face into sharp focus in my mind. That probably wasn't her voice on the tape.

At my desk, I made a mental list of the things that might be happening to me. The most obvious was that I was losing my mind. Next, I might be haunted; the voices might be ghosts. And finally, there was the conspiracy angle—someone really was sneaking into my bedroom at night and watching me sleep. But if that were true why hadn't Joanna complained about spooky visitors instead of making up a story about me snoring?

I didn't feel crazy. In fact, after the sleepless night, my mind seemed unusually sharp. Everything was bright and moist. I could see every hair on my arm. I could still taste the bacon from breakfast even if I couldn't remember eating it. I could hear my co-workers talking in low tones across the room.

There was nothing to do about the supernatural. If that was what was happening, there was no defense. That's what makes it the supernatural in the first place. It's not like an understandable force that is simply too powerful, like a bully you can overcome by pumping iron and eating your Wheaties. There is no kung fu you can do when it comes to the supernatural. It is irrational and absolutely unpredictable. If there were rules that worked, the supernatural would be science. The truly supernatural must be truly meaningless.

That only left conspiracy, but I couldn't imagine how it would be possible.

Nevertheless, my exercise in logic made me feel a little better, and in spite of the voices and in spite of a sleepless night, I got caught up in work and by early afternoon, I realized I'd forgotten all about the tape. That realization reminded me of the tape, of course, and I laughed, and everyone gave me a funny look, and I just shook my head and said, "Nothing. Sorry. Just a thought. Nothing."

For dinner, I stopped in at the same restaurant where I had had breakfast. Then I went home and wandered around the house picking things up and putting them down again. I turned on the TV.

TV was often my meditation. The challenge was to make a coherent program out of a single utterance or exclamation or exploding building or whatever from each channel. No matter what was happening, you could linger on a channel no longer than a sentence. You had to pay attention, and it took hours to get a meaningful exchange, but once I did get a something meaningful, everything fell into place. The universe became a Buddha smile, and I reached a place of blue clarity. Hours passed, and while I could not remember exactly what the experience had been about, I felt as if I'd accomplished something by the time I stopped and pushed the dirty dishes to one side so I could rinse a glass and pour a couple of fingers of scotch and put a fresh tape on the fancy recording machine in the bedroom. I could have just recorded over the old one, but I wanted to avoid ambiguity. I gulped down the scotch, brushed my teeth and undressed. I switched on the recorder, and got into bed.

"I'm going to sleep now," I said out loud so I'd have a reference point. I snuggled deeper into the covers and passed through the bed and into a dream in which all the people I had lost to death were back again, but changed. Not exactly zombies, just back and a little different. In the dream I had to make allowances for them. I'd say things like, "You'll have to excuse her, she's been dead." I'd say things like, "The way he moves certainly is *not* creepy, he was dead only yesterday." They would all come over to my house where I would feed them and teach them things and they would pretend they didn't know me and wouldn't seem the least bit grateful for my help, but I would forgive them because they'd been dead and were now trying to get back into the swing of things.

The next morning I called in sick. Judy, who took my call, wasn't surprised. "You didn't look so hot yesterday," she told me.

I popped open a beer and rewound the tape.

Forward, pause, play. Snort, moan, honk, fart, shuffle, shift, yada yada yada. Forward, pause, play.

"He's paralyzed," the woman whispered.

"How can you tell?" the man asked.

"Look at his eyes moving," she said. "There is a mechanism that paralyzes his body when he dreams. Otherwise he might get up and walk around."

The man chuckled.

"Careful with that," the woman said.

"I just need to rest," the man said.

"You shouldn't . . ."

"Shush," the man said.

She sighed. "Okay, make room for me, too," she whispered. "Careful with the covers. Okay, I'll take the front. Easy, now, easy."

"If he wakes up now," the man whispered, "he'll be looking right into your face."

"Hmmm," she said.

"Can he smell your breath?"

"Hmmm," she said.

"I'm going to pinch him."

"Don't!"

"Just joking," the man whispered.

Then nothing.

My heart was beating too fast. I listened to the silence and small night sounds until my beer was gone. I crushed the can and stood up and hit the fast-forward button.

The voices didn't occur on the tape again.

I checked all the windows and all the doors but I knew they were okay. When I got home, I always made a quick tour of the house to make sure there were no intruders lurking. I always locked the bathroom door before getting into the shower. I didn't go to bed without putting the security chain on. The movies have trained us not to make too many stupid mistakes. I had always felt secure in my own house. I'd lived there for years. I knew every inch of the place.

I went around carefully tapping all the walls looking for secret passages. I knew it was stupid. I just couldn't think of anything else to do. There was no way anyone could get in when I was asleep. How would they know when I was asleep in the first place?

I needed a second opinion. I had to let someone else listen to the tape. But who could I trust? Maybe a stranger would be better. But how would I get a stranger to listen to a tape and how could I trust what they said?

I knew who should listen to the tape. I had known from the moment I came up with the idea that someone should listen to it. I sat there staring down at my shoes, saying over and over again, "Just do it. Just do it." Okay. I got up and ran the tape back to the points just before the woman first spoke. I took it out of the machine and put it in a box and wrapped the box and addressed it to Joanna at her office. I didn't know where she was living.

I wrote a note. "Joanna, please listen to this and tell me what you hear."

I called the messenger service I sometimes used at work. An hour later the messenger arrived, and I gave him the tape and some money.

There were other things I could do while I waited. I put a fresh tape in the machine. I found a sack of flour back behind my new spices. I could spread it all over the bedroom floor and see if there were footprints in the morning. I opened the bag. But wait. If I spread the flour now, I would probably step in it many times on my way to the bathroom, which reminded me to open another beer. I took the beer and the flour into the bedroom. I put the flour down by the recorder. I would spread it just before bed. Maybe Joanna would have called before then, though. Maybe whatever she had to say would solve the problem.

"Oh, yeah," I'd say. "That's it. Boy, is my face red. I should have thought of it myself."

I could do something else, too, but it would take more courage. I could leave them a message. The danger in that was that they didn't seem to know that I could hear them. What would they do if they found out? I was completely helpless in their company. Maybe I shouldn't let them know that I knew. I was a kind of eavesdropper, really. Maybe they wouldn't like it.

They might find out anyway. One of these nights, they might notice the tape machine. And surely if I spread flour all over the floor it would tip them off.

The day passed. I ate stuff from cans for lunch. I got no reply from Joanna. I must be pretty far down on her priority list these days.

I couldn't find anything else to eat for dinner so I skipped it. There was still beer, but not too much.

RAY VUKCEVICH

I meditated with the TV for a few hours but never could achieve meaning. Around eleven I decided I really would leave them a message. It was night again and too quiet and bedtime and I had to do something. I tore a piece of paper from a notebook and wrote, "Who are you?" in big bold letters.

Now what? Should I pin it to my chest? What if they didn't find it? I wadded the paper up and tossed it in the trash.

I could write really big letters on the wall.

I dug through kitchen drawers but found nothing I could use to make big letters. I checked the bathroom. Women never leave a place without a trace. Maybe there would be a lipstick. There wasn't. So much for generalizations.

I had pink stomach stuff but it looked too runny, and I had colorless roll-on deodorant, so the wall wouldn't sweat, but you'd have to smell the country fresh letters to puzzle out the message.

Ah ha. An old old bottle of tincture of merthiolate. Good god, I bought that before I met Abby. What was the expiration date? Most of the label was gone, but it looked like 1980. I had put the stuff on countless cuts. It still had a nice sting to it. This was one of those products that one bottle lasts you a lifetime. The company had probably gone out of business.

I stood on the bed and, using the little plastic applicator, started my message again on the wall. Rats. The applicator was too small. It would take forever. I poured merthiolate into my hand and smacked my hand onto the wall and dragged it down and up and down and up in a big dripping orange double-u. Okay. The rest went pretty quickly.

Who are you?

If they looked at me, and I seemed to be pretty much all they did look at, they could not fail to see my message.

My hands were orange. The orange stain wouldn't come off with soap and water. To hell with it.

246

How about the flour?

Okay, okay. But do it carefully. Get undressed first. Start at the bathroom door and work your way back to the bed. Yes, like that. When you get to the bed just toss the empty flour sack out of the bedroom and get into bed. That's it. Nothing could move across there without leaving a mark. Good. Good. Goddamn it, you forgot to pee.

I plopped down on the bed. I tossed the empty flour sack over the side. I took a deep breath. Then I walked straight across the flour to the bathroom. One straight path. I would use the same one coming back. Anything off that path would be my visitors.

Except that after I used the bathroom and carefully walked back to the bed, I realized I would need one more path to the dresser so I could turn on the recorder. Okay, one more. I walked to the dresser, turned on the machine, and walked back to the bed. Two paths. Footprints going in both directions. I got into bed.

I stared up at the ceiling, feeling like an absolute idiot. I would have to get up and make another path if I wanted to turn off the light. I got up and walked to the light switch and flipped it off. Then I made my way back in the dark. I knew I was not keeping a straight path. And as I walked, it occurred to me to wonder how they would see my message in the dark. I had probably ruined the wall for nothing. I stopped and closed my eyes to think about it. If they could see me, they could probably see the wall, but what about the orange letters? Would orange letters be visible to ghosts who could see in the dark? Maybe it would be like red light to fish. You put a red light in your aquarium and the fish all think it's night and you can watch them and they don't know you're watching.

I opened my eyes and stumbled forward and saw the street glow through the bathroom window and realized that I'd gotten way off the path back to the bed. The flour seemed mostly pointless now.

I turned, and then stood peering through the dark at the bed. It didn't look entirely empty. Those shapes could be my pillows. The slight movement I saw, like the quivering of a horse after a good run, might be just the kind of thing you see in the dark. I took a step back.

"Aren't you coming to bed," she said.

I cried out.

"Sorry, I didn't mean to startle you."

"Joanna?"

"I heard the tape of you snoring," she whispered. "Kind of a strange apology, but what the hell. Come on, hop in. It's late."

I sat down on the edge of the bed. She put her cool hand on my shoulder. I crawled in beside her. She pulled me in close.

"Is that really you, Joanna?" I asked.

"Of course, it isn't, you moron," the man behind me said.

MEET ME IN THE MOON ROOM

M aybe we'll meet again on the moon," she said, and it hadn't sounded so strange in 1967, hadn't been altogether out of the question. It was just another one of those impossible things we dealt with before breakfast in 1967.

"And when do you expect this meeting to happen?" I asked.

"Give us thirty years to mellow," she said. "We'll have a solstice reunion in the nineties."

I'd had a lot more hair in those days, and a slimmer, trimmer prostate, flat if not exactly rippling abs, endless optimism. I was her rocket man, nerdy before nerdy was cool, and I always embarrassed her in front of her friends. Louisa, whom everyone called the Star Girl, wore flowers in her hair and bellbottoms, and I undressed her in my mind every 15.7 seconds.

I wondered if she would expect me to call her the Star Woman tonight.

"You could come with me," she said in 1967.

But, of course, I couldn't. No way I would have thrown away a career in space to do dharma in Tangiers. We'd been a cacophony of becoming, the two of us, but I'd fooled myself into thinking I knew exactly where I was going.

"You could stay with me," I said.

"I'm already gone," she said. "You're talking to an afterimage."

Several years later, just after the first lunar landing, I heard she'd been killed in North Africa. I didn't want to know the details.

Then one foggy Christmas Eve, Louisa called me up to say, "Meet me in the Moon Room."

Right out of the blue.

"Not out of the blue," she said. "It's our thirty-year solstice reunion. Don't tell me you've forgotten."

"I haven't forgotten," I said. "But what the hell is the Moon Room?"

"It's on the West Side." She gave me the address and hung up. For a long time I stood there looking at the phone wondering if I'd made her up.

Then I got in the car and drove though the mostly empty streets to a neighborhood I would not have come to voluntarily. Most of the buildings looked deserted. Half the streetlights were dead. The only other car I saw passed me and the driver gave me a dark and sullen look like he was sizing me up for a mugging. If I'd been in a movie, my headlights would have surprised a dirty white dog skulking out of an alley with the bloody remains of someone's arm in its mouth.

I finally found the address Louisa had given me. The building looked like an airplane hanger. Metal walls and big windows with many small square panes of cloudy white glass set up way too high for anyone to actually look out of them. A crudely lettered sign nailed onto a wooden door that didn't quite fit its doorway said, THE MOON ROOM—WELCOME ABOARD!

I pushed open the door and peered into the darkness.

"Go on through," someone said, a man.

I sucked in my breath and stepped to one side, but didn't embarrass myself with a yelp. "What?"

"Through the airlock," he said. I still couldn't see him.

"The airlock?"

"Here." He moved out of the shadows, beer, sweat, and peppermint, and I heard the distinctive sound of Velcro being separated. Noise and light flowed from a slash in the darkness.

"Thanks," I said and stepped through into a huge bright space. The building was one big room, many stories tall, with track lighting. My first thought was that the place was full of people swinging from vines while dark monkeys perched far above them on metal girders.

I looked across a lunar landscape of scattered gray moon rocks and craters with starched Stars and Stripes, like flags marking golfing holes, to a huge blue Earth on the far wall.

"We are all gazelles in the Moon Room," the man who had showed me in said, and zipped up the airlock. I never did see his face.

Elastic straps—perhaps bungee cords, perhaps not—depended from the ceiling and attached to harnesses worn by all the patrons of the Moon Room. They weren't swinging from vines. They were moon walking—big steps, long leaps, getting from here to there in an unearthly hurry.

But those really were monkeys up there—howler monkeys. I could hear them now.

"We also suck strong drink from plastic bottles with plastic straws."

I turned to the voice and saw Louisa bobbing up and down in her harness—definitely Louisa, big grin and fuzzy red hair, baggy jeans and tie-dye, holding a couple of squeeze bottles. "Get hooked up." She tossed me one of the bottles and jumped away like a deer—or more like, I suppose, a middle-aged woman on the moon.

Someone came putt-putting up to me in a lunar rover. Her nametag said, HI, I'M RITA!

"Hi, Rita," I said.

"Ho ho," she said and plopped a floppy red Santa hat onto my head. "Here, your harness goes like this." She took the drink from my hand and helped me get into my harness.

"Why the howler monkeys?" I asked.

"Not what you expected, hey?" She gave me my drink back, put her hand flat against my chest, and pushed me onto the moon.

I jumped around like crazy, slurping what turned out to be rum and coke, looking for Louisa, but when I found her I was suddenly shy. What could I say after all these years? How could I break the ice? "Did you know," I said, "that the chances of being attacked by a hippo are really quite small?"

She laughed the clear crystal laugh I remembered so well. "As it happens," she said, "I really do know that!"

"Amazing," I said. But it wasn't really so amazing. Of course she would know that. She would have learned many things on her travels around the world while I was selling insurance in the seventies and teaching high school in the eighties and coding COBOL as a resurrected relic working on the year 2000 problem in the nineties. I imagined her skiing and skydiving and hobnobbing with witch doctors. She would have been chasing lions in a jeep while I paid off the Ford.

"So, did you ever get into orbit?" she asked.

"No," I said. "Did you ever manage to meet Paul Bowles?"

"Actually, I did," she said, "and thanks for not asking about the book."

She meant the Great American Novel she'd run off to North Africa to write.

"Are you a ghost, Louisa?" I asked.

"Touch me and see," she said softly, and I reached for her, but nothing is easy on the moon. Especially not when the place is crowded with desperate drinking people bouncing around doing the bunny hop, singing Christmas songs, forming and dissolving conga lines. Louisa was swept away. I bounded after her.

Elbowing my way through all the lunatics looking for lost dreams, I managed to grab her. I turned her and we sat facing one another in our harnesses. I put my hand on her knee.

"Not there," she said, but I didn't let go. Her knee was metal or plastic or both.

And then I'm thinking that she's thinking that I'm thinking I would ask her to come home with me now out of some misplaced sense of obligation to the past we had once shared.

A hard look came to her face, and she took my other hand and put it on her other knee. It was artificial, too.

"Tangiers?" I asked.

"Tangiers," she said.

And I'm thinking that she's thinking that I'm desperately looking for some excuse to end this right here, right now, but what I'm really thinking is how hard it is to know what to do next after you've finally figured out the meaning of life, after you've seen it's all nothing more than a couple of people huddling close for comfort in a cold universe.

I couldn't let her go again.

Her expression softened.

And I'm thinking that she's thinking that she really does know what I'm thinking.

She squeezed my hands on her knees and said, "Okay."

Ray Vukcevich was born in Carlsbad, New Mexico, and grew up in the Southwest. He now lives in Eugene and works as a computer programmer in a couple of brain labs at the University of Oregon. His short fiction has appeared in many magazines and anthologies, including *Asimov's*, *Twists of the Tale*, *The Magazine of Fantasy & Science Fiction*, *Rosebud*, and *Pulphouse*. His first novel, *The Man of Maybe Half-a-Dozen Faces*, was published in 2000 by St. Martin's Press.

:PUBLICATION HISTORY:

These stories were previously published as follows: The Barber's Theme, *Sirius*Visions*, 1995; A Breath Holding Contest, *Pulphouse*, 1991; By the Time We Get to Uranus, *Imagination Fully Dilated*, ed. Alan M. Clark & Elizabeth Engstrom, 1998; Catch, *Twists of the Tale*, ed. Ellen Datlow, 1996; Ceremony, *Pulphouse*, 1991; Doing Time, *Pulphouse*, 1992; Fancy Pants, *Imagination Fully Dilated*, Volume II, edited by Elizabeth Engstrom, 2000; Finally Fruit, *The Urbanite*, 1997; The Finger, *The Magazine of Fantasy and Science Fiction (F&SF)*, 1995; Giant Step, *F&SF*, 1994; A Holiday Junket, *F&SF*, 1998; Home Remedy, *Talebones*, 1996; Meet Me in the Moon Room, *Rosebud*, 1998; Mom's Little Friends, *F&SF*, 1992; My Mustache, *Asimov's*, 1993; The Next Best Thing, *Talebones*, 1998; No Comet, *F&SF*, 1994; The Perfect Gift, *Asimov's*, 1994; Poop, *F&SF*, 2000; Pretending, *Lady Churchill's Rosebud Wristlet*, 2001; Quite Contrary, *Pulphouse*, 1994; Rejoice, *F&SF*, 1999; Season Finale, *Pulphouse*, 1995; There Is Danger, *Pulphouse*, 1993; We Kill a Bicycle, *VB Tech Journal*, 1995; Whisper, *F&SF*, 2001; White Guys in Space, *F&SF*, 1996.

:Acknowledgements:

With thanks to Dean Wesley Smith and Kristine Kathryn Rusch who were there for me early on. Thanks to Damon Knight and Kate Wilhelm for wise words and wonderful examples. And thanks to good friends who fed and drove me around during a mostly blind summer: Jerry Oltion, Leslie What, Nina Kiriki Hoffman, Bruce Holland Rogers, Holly Arrow, Alan Roberts, and Rob Vagle. Not to mention all the folks who come and go at the Tuesday night workshop, and Diana Blackmon, Tom Lindell, and Nicole Brown, who slipped through the cracks last time.